Acting Edition

Trouble

by Alice Childress

ǁ SAMUEL FRENCH ǁ

ISBN 978-0-573-70996-8

www.concordtheatricals.com
www.concordtheatricals.co.uk

FOR PRODUCTION INQUIRIES
UNITED STATES AND CANADA
info@concordtheatricals.com
1-866-979-0447

UNITED KINGDOM AND EUROPE
licensing@concordtheatricals.co.uk
020-7054-7298

Each title is subject to availability from Concord Theatricals Corp.,
depending upon country of performance. Please be aware that
TROUBLE IN MIND may not be licensed by Concord Theatricals Corp.
in your territory. Professional and amateur producers should contact
the nearest Concord Theatricals Corp. office or licensing partner to
verify availability.

This work is published by Samuel French, an imprint of Concord
Theatricals Corp.

No one shall make any changes in this title(s) for the purpose of production. No part of this book may be reproduced, stored in a retrieval system, scanned, uploaded, or transmitted in any form, by any means, now known or yet to be invented, including mechanical, electronic, digital, photocopying, recording, videotaping, or otherwise, without the prior written permission of the publisher. No one shall share this title(s), or any part of this title(s), through any social media or file hosting websites.

For all inquiries regarding motion picture, television, online/digital and other media rights, please contact Concord Theatricals Corp.

MUSIC AND THIRD-PARTY MATERIALS USE NOTE

Licensees are solely responsible for obtaining formal written permission from copyright owners to use copyrighted music and/or other copyrighted third-party materials (e.g., artworks, logos) in the performance of this play and are strongly cautioned to do so. If no such permission is obtained by the licensee, then the licensee must use only original music and materials that the licensee owns and controls. Licensees are solely responsible and liable for clearances of all third-party copyrighted materials, including without limitation music, and shall indemnify the copyright owners of the play(s) and their licensing agent, Concord Theatricals Corp., against any costs, expenses, losses and liabilities arising from the use of such copyrighted third-party materials by licensees. For music, please contact the appropriate music licensing authority in your territory for the rights to any incidental music.

IMPORTANT BILLING AND CREDIT REQUIREMENTS

If you have obtained performance rights to this title, please refer to your licensing agreement for important billing and credit requirements.

TROUBLE IN MIND opened on Broadway at the American Airlines Theatre on November 18, 2021, produced by Roundabout Theatre Company (Todd Haimes, Artistic Director/CEO; Julia C. Levy, Executive Director; Sydney Beers, Executive Producer; Steve Dow, Chief Administrative Officer). The production was directed by Charles Randolph-Wright, with scenic design by Arnulfo Maldonado, costume design by Emilio Sosa, lighting design by Kathy A. Perkins, sound design by Dan Moses Schreier, hair and wigs by Cookie Jordan, makeup by Kirk Cambridge-Del Pesche, and original music by Nona Hendryx. The stage manager was Alfredo Macias. The cast was as follows:

WILETTA MAYER	LaChanze
HENRY	Simon Jones
JOHN NEVINS	Brandon Micheal Hall
MILLIE DAVIS	Jessica Frances Dukes
JUDY SEARS	Danielle Campbell
SHELDON FORRESTER	Chuck Cooper
AL MANNERS	Michael Zegen
EDDIE FENTON	Alex Mickiewicz
BILL O'WRAY	Don Stephenson

TROUBLE IN MIND opened at the Greenwich Mews Theatre (Lily Turner, Artistic Director; Stella Holt, Administrative Coordinator) on November 4, 1955 in New York City and ran for ninety-one performances. The play was directed by Clarice Taylor and Alice Childress. The scenic and lighting design were by Vincent Sorrentino. The stage manager was Howard Augusta. The cast was as follows:

WILETTA MAYER	Clarice Taylor
POP [HENRY]	Liam Lenihan
JOHN NEVILLE [NEVINS]	Charles Bettis
MILLIE DAVIS	Hilda Haynes
JUDITH SEARS	Stephanie Elliot
SHELDON FORRESTER	Howard Augusta
AL MANNERS	James McMahon
EDDIE FENTON	Hal England
HOODAN [BILL O'WRAY]	Johnny Barracuda
SINGER	Louise Kemp

CHARACTERS

WILETTA MAYER – Black woman, middle-aged

HENRY – White man, elderly

JOHN NEVINS – Black man, young

MILLIE DAVIS – Black woman, about thirty-five years old

JUDY SEARS – White woman, young

SHELDON FORRESTER – Black man, elderly

AL MANNERS – White man, early forties

EDDIE FENTON – White man

BILL O'WRAY – White man

SETTING

A Broadway theater in New York City

TIME

1957

NOTE ON CASTING

Licensees should do their best to cast each character in accordance with the race, gender, and age specified in each character description.

ACT I

(A Broadway theater in New York City. Ten o'clock Monday morning. Fall 1957. Blues music in, out after lights up.)*

(The stage of the theater. Stage left leads to the outside entrance, stage right to upstairs dressing rooms.)

(There are many props and leftovers from the last show: a plaster fountain with a cupid perched atop, garden furniture, tables, benches, a trellis, two white armchairs trimmed with gold gilt.)

(Before the curtain rises, we hear banging sounds from offstage left. The banging grows louder and louder.)

(Curtain rises. **WILETTA MAYER,** *a middle-aged actress, appears. She is attractive and expansive in personality. She carries a purse and a script. At the moment, she is in quite a huff.)*

WILETTA. My Lord, I like to have wore my arm off bangin' on that door! What you got it locked for?

(Lights up brighter.)

---

*A license to produce *Trouble in Mind* does not include a performance license for any third-party or copyrighted music. Licensees should create an original composition or use music in the public domain. For further information, please see the Music and Third-Party Materials Use Note on page iii.

1

WILETTA. Had me standin' out there in the cold, catchin' my death of pneumonia!

> (**HENRY,** *the elderly doorman, enters.*)

HENRY. I didn't hear a thing... I didn't know...

> (**WILETTA** *is suddenly moved by the sight of the theater. She holds up her hand for silence, looks out and up at the balcony. She loves the theater. She turns back to* **HENRY.**)

WILETTA. A theater always makes me feel that way...gotta get still for a second.

HENRY. (*Welcomes an old memory.*) You...you are Wiletta Mayer...more than twenty years ago, in the old Galy Theater...

> (**WILETTA** *is pleased to be remembered.*)

You was singin' a number, with the lights changin' color all around you... What was the name of that show?

WILETTA. *Brownskin Melody.*

HENRY. That's it...and the lights...

WILETTA. Was a doggone rainbow.

HENRY. And you looked so pretty and sounded so fine, there's no denyin' it.

WILETTA. Thank you, but I... I...

> (**WILETTA** *hates to admit she doesn't remember him.*)

HENRY. I'm Henry.

WILETTA. Mmmmm, you don't say.

HENRY. I was the electrician. Rigged up all those lights and never missed a cue. I'm the doorman here now. I've been in show business over fifty years. I'm the doorman... Henry.

WILETTA. That's a nice name. I... I sure remember those lights.

HENRY. Bet you can't guess how old I am, I'll betcha.

WILETTA. *(Would rather not guess.)* Well...you're sure lookin' good.

HENRY. Go ahead, take a guess.

WILETTA. *(Being very kind.)* Ohhhhh, I'd say you're in your...late fifties.

HENRY. *(Laughs proudly.)* I fool 'em all! I'm seventy-eight years old! How's that?

WILETTA. Ohhhh, don't be tellin' it.

> *(She places her script and purse on the table, removes her coat.* **HENRY** *takes her coat and hangs it on a rack.)*

HENRY. You singin' in this new show?

WILETTA. No, I'm actin'. I play the mother.

HENRY. *(Hard of hearing.)* How's that?

WILETTA. I'm the mother!

HENRY. Could I run next door and get you some coffee? I'm goin' anyway, no bother.

WILETTA. No, thank you just the same.

HENRY. If you open here, don't let 'em give you dressin' room "C." It's small and it's got no "john" in it...excuse me, I mean...no commode... Miss Mayer.

WILETTA. *(Feeling like the star he's made her.)* Thank you, I'll watch out for that.

> *(***HENRY*** *reaches for a small chair, changes his mind, and draws the gilt armchair to the table.)*

HENRY. Make yourself comfortable. The old Galy. Yessir, I'm seventy-eight years old.

WILETTA. Well, I'm not gonna tell you my age. A woman that'll tell her age will tell anything.

HENRY. *(Laughs.)* Oh, that's a good one! I'll remember that! A woman that'll tell her age...what else?

WILETTA. Will tell anything.

HENRY. *Will* tell. Well, I'll see you a little later.

> *(He exits stage left.)*

WILETTA. *(Saying goodbye to the kind of gentle treatment she seldom receives.)* So long.

> *(She rises and walks downstage, strikes a pose from the "old Galy," and sings a snatch of an old song.)*

OH, HONEY BABE
OH, HONEY BABE...

> *(She pushes the memory aside.)*

Yes, indeed!

> *(**JOHN NEVINS,** a young Black actor, enters. He tries to look self-assured, but it's obvious that he is new to the theater and fighting hard to control his enthusiasm.)*

Good morning. Another early bird! I'm glad they hired you, you read so nice er...ah...

JOHN. John, John Nevins.

WILETTA. This is new for you, ain't it?

JOHN. Yes, ma'am.

WILETTA. Yes, ma'am? I know you're not a New Yorker, where's your home?

JOHN. Newport News, that's in Virginia.

WILETTA. HOT DOG. I shoulda known anyone as handsome and mannerly as you had to come from my home. Newport News! Think of that! Last name?

JOHN. Nevins, John Nevins.

WILETTA. Wait a minute...do you know Estelle Nevins, used to live out on Prairie Road...fine-built woman?

JOHN. Guess I do, that's my mother.

WILETTA. *(Very touched.)* No, she ain't!

JOHN. *(Afraid of oncoming sentiment.)* Yes...ah...yes she is.

WILETTA. What a day! I went to school with Estelle! She married a fella named Clarence! Used to play baseball. Last time I hit home she had a little baby in the carriage. How many children she got?

JOHN. I'm the only one.

WILETTA. You can't be that little baby in the carriage! Stand up, let me look at you! Brings all of yesterday back to my mind! Tell me, John, is the drugstore still on the corner? Used to be run by a tall, strappin' fella... got wavy, black hair...and, well, he's kind of devilish... Eddie Bentley!

JOHN. Oh yes, Mr. Bentley is still there...

WILETTA. Fresh and sassy and...

JOHN. But he's gray-haired and very stern and businesslike.

WILETTA. *(Very conscious of her age.)* You don't say. Why you want to act? Why don't you make somethin' outta yourself?

JOHN. *(Amazed at this.)* What? Well, I...

WILETTA. You look bright enough to be a doctor or even a lawyer maybe... You don't have to take what I've been through...don't have to take it off 'em.

JOHN. I think the theater is the grandest place in the world, and I plan to go right to the top.

WILETTA. *(With good humor.)* Uh-huh, and where do you think I was plannin' to go?

JOHN. *(Feeling slightly superior because he thinks he knows more about the craft than* **WILETTA.***)* Ohhh, well...

WILETTA. *(Quick to sense his feelings.)* Oh, well, what?

JOHN. *(Feels a bit chastised.)* Nothing. I know what I want to do. I'm set, decided, and that's that. You're in it, aren't you proud to be a part of it all?

WILETTA. Of what all?

JOHN. Theater.

WILETTA. *Show business*, it's just a business. Colored folks ain't in no theater. You ever do a professional show before?

JOHN. Yes, some Off-Broadway...and I've taken classes.

WILETTA. Don't let the man know that. They don't like us to go to school.

JOHN. Oh, now.

WILETTA. They want us to be naturals...you know, just born with the gift. 'Course they want you to be experienced too. Tell 'em you was in the last revival of *Porgy and Bess*.

JOHN. I'm a little young for that.

WILETTA. They don't know the difference. You were one of the children.

JOHN. I need this job but...must I lie?

WILETTA. Yes. Management hates folks who *need* jobs. They get the least money, the least respect, and most times they don't get the job.

JOHN. *(Laughs.)* Got it. I'm always doing great.

WILETTA. But don't get too cocky. They don't like that either. You have to cater to these fools too...

JOHN. I'm afraid I don't know how to do that.

WILETTA. Laugh! Laugh at everything they say, makes 'em feel superior.

JOHN. Why do they have to feel superior?

WILETTA. You gonna sit there and pretend you don't know why?

JOHN. I... I'd feel silly laughing at everything.

WILETTA. You don't. Sometimes they laugh, you're supposed to look serious, other times they serious, you supposed to laugh.

JOHN. *(In polite disagreement.)* Sounds too complicated.

WILETTA. *(Warming to her subject.)* Nothin' to it. Suppose the director walks in, looks around, and says... *(Mimics Al Manners.)* "Well, if the dust around here doesn't choke us to death, we'll be able to freeze in comfort."

JOHN. Yes?

WILETTA. We laugh and dispute him. *(Illustrates.)* "Oh, now, Mr. Manners, it ain't that bad!" ...White folks can't stand unhappy Negroes...so laugh, laugh when it ain't funny at all.

JOHN. Sounds kind of Uncle Tommish.

WILETTA. You callin' me a "Tom"?

JOHN. No, ma'am.

WILETTA. Stop sayin' ma'am, it sounds countrified.

JOHN. Yes.

WILETTA. It is Tommish...but they do it more than we do. They call it bein' a "yes man." You either do it and stay

or don't do it and get out. I can let you in on things that
school never heard of...'cause I know what's out here
and they don't.

JOHN. Thank you. I guess I'll learn the ropes as I go along.

WILETTA. I'm tellin' you now! Oh, you so lucky! Nobody
told me, had to learn it for myself.

> (**JOHN** *is trying to hide the fact that he does
> not relish her instructions.*)

Another thing. He's gonna ask your honest opinion
about the play. Don't tell him, he don't mean it...just
say you're crazy about it...butter him up.

> (*This remark really bothers* **JOHN**.)

JOHN. What *do* you think of our play?

WILETTA. Oh, honey, it stinks, ain't nothin' at all. 'Course, if
I hear that again, I'll swear you lyin'.

JOHN. Why are you doing it? A flop can't make you but
so rich.

WILETTA. Who said it's gonna flop? I said it ain't nothin',
but things that aggravate me always *run* for a long
time...'cause what bugs me is what sends somebody
else, if you know what I mean.

JOHN. (*Defensively.*) I studied it thoroughly and...

WILETTA. Honey, don't study it, just learn it.

JOHN. I wouldn't, couldn't play anything I didn't believe
in...I couldn't.

WILETTA. (*Understands he's a bit upstage now.*) Oh, well,
you just a lost ball in the high grass.

> (**MILLIE DAVIS**, *a Black actress about thirty-
> five years old, enters. She breezes in, beautifully
> dressed in a mink coat, pastel wool dress and
> hat, suede shoes, and bag.*)

MILLIE. Hi!

WILETTA. Walk, girl! Don't she look good?

MILLIE. Don't look too hard, it's not paid for.

> *(She models the coat for* **WILETTA** *as she talks to* **JOHN***.)*

You got the job! Good for you.

> *(***WILETTA** *picks up* **MILLIE***'s newspaper.)*

JOHN. And congratulations to you.

> *(***MILLIE** *takes off her coat and hangs it up.)*

MILLIE. I don't care one way or the other 'cause my husband doesn't want me workin' anyway.

WILETTA. Is he still a dining-car waiter?

MILLIE. I wanted to read for your part but Mr. Manners said I was too young. They always say too young...too young.

WILETTA. Hear they're lookin' for a little girl to play Goldilocks, maybe you should try for that.

MILLIE. Oh, funny.

WILETTA. *(Commenting on the headlines.)* Look at 'em! Throwin' stones at little children, got to call out the militia to go to school.

JOHN. That's terrible.

MILLIE. *(Quite proud of her contribution to Little Rock.)* A woman pushed me on the subway this mornin' and I was ready for her! Called her everything but a child of God. She turned purple! Oh, I fixed her!

> *(***JUDY SEARS**, *a young actress [white], is heard offstage with* **SHELDON FORRESTER**, *an elderly Black character man.)*

JUDY. *(Offstage.)* This way...

SHELDON. *(Offstage.)* Yes, ma'am. Don't hurt yourself.

> *(SHELDON and JUDY enter, JUDY first.)*

JUDY. Good morning.

> *(Others respond in unison.)*

JOHN. Hello again, glad you made it.

MILLIE. Hi! I'm Millie, that's John, Wiletta, and you're?

JUDY. Judith, just call me Judy.

> *(SHELDON is bundled in a heavy overcoat and two scarves, one outer, one inner.)*

SHELDON. And call me Shel!

WILETTA. Sheldon Forrester! So glad to see you! Heard you was sick.

MILLIE. I heard he was dead.

SHELDON. Yes! Some fool wrote a piece in that *Medium Brown Magazine* 'bout me bein' dead. You can see he was lyin'. But I lost a lotta work on accounta that. Doctor says that with plenty of rest and fresh air, I oughta outlive him.

WILETTA. Bet you will, too.

SHELDON. Mr. Manners was lookin' all over for me, said nobody could play this part but me.

MILLIE. Not another soul can do what you're gonna do to it.

SHELDON. Thank you.

> *(JOHN starts over to JUDY, but SHELDON stops him.)*

Didn't you play in er...ah...er...

WILETTA. He was in the last revival of *Porgy and Bess*. Was one of the children.

*(She watches **JOHN**'s reaction to this.)*

SHELDON. Yeah, I know I remembered you. He ain't changed much, just bigger. Nice little actor.

JOHN. *(Embarrassed.)* Thank you, sir.

WILETTA. Sheldon got a good memory.

MILLIE. *(To **JUDY**.)* What're you doing?

SHELDON. She's *Miss* Renard, the southerner's daughter. Fights her father 'bout the way he's treatin' us.

MILLIE. What I want is a part where I get to fight him.

WILETTA. Ha! That'll be the day!

SHELDON. Bill O'Wray is the father, he's awful nice.

MILLIE. Also wish I'd get to wear some decent clothes sometime. Only chance I get to dress up is offstage. I'll wear them baggy cotton dresses but damn if I'll wear another bandana.

SHELDON. That's how country people do! But go on the beach today, what do you see? Bandanas. White folks wear 'em! They stylish!

MILLIE. That's a lot of crap! –

SHELDON. There you go! You holler when there's no work – when the man give you some, you holler just as loud. Ain't no pleasin' you!

> *(**JOHN** starts toward **JUDY** again; this time **MILLIE** stops him.)*

MILLIE. Last show I was in, I wouldn't even tell my relatives. All I did was shout, "Lord, have mercy!" for almost two hours every night.

WILETTA. Yes, but you did it, so hush! She's played every flower in the garden. Let's see, what was your name in that TV mess?

MILLIE. Never mind.

WILETTA. Gardenia! She was Gardenia! 'Nother thing...she was Magnolia, Chrysanthemum was another...

MILLIE. And you've done the jewels...Crystal, Pearl, Opal!

> (**MILLIE** *laughs.*)

JOHN. *(Weak, self-conscious laughter.)* Oh, now...

> (**JUDY** *has retreated to one side, trying to hide herself behind a book.*)

SHELDON. Do, Lord, let's keep the peace. Last thing I was in, the folks fought and argued so, the man said he'd never do a colored show again...and he didn't!

WILETTA. I always say it's the man's play, the man's money, and the man's theater, so what you gonna do? *(To* **MILLIE.***)* You ain't got a pot nor a window. Now, when you get your own...

> (**SHELDON** *clears his throat to remind them that* **JUDY** *is listening.*)

Honey, er...what you say your name was?

JUDY. Judy.

> (**WILETTA** *sweeps over to* **JUDY** *and tries to cover the past argument.*)

WILETTA. I know I've seen you in pictures, didn't you make some pictures?

JUDY. No, this is my first job.

JOHN. *(Joshing* **WILETTA.***)* Oh, you mustn't tell that because –

WILETTA. *(Cutting him off.)* You're just as cute as a new penny.

SHELDON. Sure is.

> *(A brief moment of silence while they wait for* **JUDY** *to say something.)*

JUDY. *(Starts hesitantly, but picks up momentum as she goes along.)* Thank you, and er...er...I hope I can do a good job and that people learn something from this play.

MILLIE. Like what?

JUDY. That people are the same, that people are...are... well, you know...that people are people.

SHELDON. There you go...brotherhood of man stuff! Sure!

WILETTA. Yes, indeed. I don't like to think of theater as just a business. Oh, it's the art...ain't art a wonderful thing?

MILLIE. *(Bald, fat statement to no one in particular.)* People aren't the same.

JUDY. I read twice for the part and there were so many others before me and after me...and I was so scared that my voice came out all funny... I stumbled on the rug when I went in...everything was terrible.

MILLIE. *(Another bald, fat statement.)* But you got the job.

JUDY. *(Uneasy about* **MILLIE***'s attitude.)* Yes.

JOHN. *(To the rescue.)* And all the proud relatives will cheer you on opening night!

JUDY. *(Nothing can drown her spirits for long.)* Yes! My mother and father...they live in Bridgeport...they really don't want me here at all. They keep expecting something *terrible* to happen to me...like being murdered or something! But they're awfully sweet and they'll be so happy. *(Abrupt change of subject.)* What do you think of the play?

WILETTA. Oh, I never had anything affect me so much in all my life. It's so sad, ain't it sad?

JUDY. Oh, there's some humor.

WILETTA. I'm tellin' you, I almost busted my sides laughin'.

(**SHELDON** *is busy looking in the script.*)

JOHN. It has a social theme and something to say.

JUDY. Yes.

WILETTA. Art! Art is a great thing!

MILLIE. It's all right except for a few words here and there... and those gawd-awful clothes...

JOHN. Words, clothes. What about the very meaning?

(**SHELDON** *startles everyone by reading out loud. His finger runs down the page; he skips his cues and reads his lines.*)

SHELDON. Mr. Renard, sir, everything is just fine... Yes, sir... Thank you, sir... Yes, sireee, I sure will... I know... Yes, sir... But iffen, iffen...

(*He pauses to question the word.*)

Iffen?

(*Now he understands.*)

Iffen you don't mind, we'd like to use the barn.

MILLIE. Iffen.

SHELDON. Hush, Millie, so I can get these lines, I'm not a good reader, you know.

MILLIE. Iffen you forget one, just keep shakin' your head.

(*Offstage we hear a door slam.* **AL MANNERS**, *the director [white], is giving* **EDDIE FENTON**, *the stage manager [white], a friendly chastising.*)

MANNERS. (*Offstage.*) Eddie, why? Why do you do it?

EDDIE. *(Offstage.)* I didn't know.

SHELDON. *(Assumes a very studious air and begins to study his script earnestly.)* Mr. Manners.

> *(***EDDIE** *and* **MANNERS** *enter, followed by* **HENRY.** **EDDIE** *is eager and quick. He carries a portfolio and a stack of scripts.* **MANNERS** *is in his early forties, hatless, a well-tweeded product of Hollywood. He is a bundle of energy, considerate and understanding after his own fashion; selfish and tactless after ours.* **HENRY** *is following him around, ready to write out a coffee order.)*

EDDIE. *(With a smile.)* You asked my opinion.

MANNERS. That, my friend, was a mistake.

EDDIE. *(Laughing while the* **CAST** *smiles in anticipation of* **MANNERS'** *words.)* Okay, I admit you were right, you were.

MANNERS. *(Enjoying himself.)* Of course I was. *(To* **CAST.***)* All of his taste is in his mouth!

> *(Burst of* **CAST** *laughter, especially from* **SHELDON** *and* **WILETTA.***)*

EDDIE. *(Playfully correcting* **MANNERS.***)* All right, Al, play fair...uncle...a truce.

MANNERS. *(To* **CAST.***)* Greetings to New York's finest.

CAST. *(Ad-lib.)* Good morning... Flatterer... Hello... Good morning.

MANNERS. *(To* **HENRY.***)* Coffee all around the room and count yourself in.

> *(He hands* **HENRY** *a bill.)*

Rolls? Cake? No...how about danish...all right?

CAST. *(Ad-lib.)* Yes... Sure... Anything... Okay.

SHELDON. I like doughnuts, those jelly doughnuts.

MANNERS. Jelly doughnuts! What a horrible thought. Get danish...all right?

CAST. *(Ad-lib.)* Sure... Anything... That's fine.

MANNERS. *(After* **HENRY** *exits.)* If you were looking for that type, you could never find it! A real character.

JOHN. One of the old forty-niners.

MANNERS. No, no...not quite that...

> *(He turns off that faucet and quickly switches to another.)*

Everyone on speaking terms?

CAST. *(Ad-lib.)* Of course... Old friends... Oh, yes... Sure.

> *(****MANNERS*** *opens the portfolio with a flourish.)*

MANNERS. Best scenic design you've ever laid eyes on.

> *(All gasp and sigh as they gather around him. They are quite impressed with the sketch.* **JUDY** *is very close, and* **MANNERS** *looks down at her hair and neck, which is perched right under his nostrils.* **JUDY** *can feel his breath on her neck. She turns suddenly, and* **MANNERS** *backs away a trifle.)*

You er...wear a beautiful dress in the third act and I wanted to see if you have nice shoulders.

> *(****JUDY*** *backs away slightly.)*

I wasn't planning to attack you.

> *(The* **CAST** *laughs.)*

MILLIE. I got nice shoulders. You got one of those dresses for me?

SHELDON. *(Determined to enjoy everything.)* Ha! He wasn't gonna attack her!

MANNERS. *(Suddenly changes faucets again.)* Oh, I'm so weary.

EDDIE. *(Running interference.)* He was with Melton on this sketch until four a.m.

MANNERS. Four-thirty.

EDDIE. Four-thirty.

MANNERS. *(Swoops down on* **WILETTA***.)* Ahhhhh, this is my sweetheart!

WILETTA. *(With mock severity.)* Go on! Go 'way! Ain't speakin' to you! He won't eat, he won't sleep, he's just terrible! I'm mad with you.

SHELDON. Gonna ruin your health like that!

WILETTA. Gonna kill himself!

MANNERS. Bawl me out, I deserve it.

EDDIE. Melton is so stubborn, won't change a line.

MANNERS. But he did.

EDDIE. Yes, but so stubborn.

MANNERS. A genius should be stubborn. *(Pointing index finger at* **SHELDON***.)* Right?

SHELDON. *(Snaps his fingers and points back.)* There you go!

(The **CAST** *laughs.)*

MANNERS. *(To* **WILETTA***.)* You'd better speak to me. This is my girl, we did a picture together.

CAST. *(Ad-lib.)* Really?... How nice... She sure did... That's right.

MANNERS. *(As though it's been centuries.)* Ohhhhhh, years and years ago.

MILLIE. *(To* **WILETTA.***)* Remember that?

MANNERS. He and I worked together too.

SHELDON. *(Proudly.)* I was helpin' the Confederate Army.

MANNERS. And what a chestnut: guns, cannons, drums, Indians, slaves, hearts and flowers, sex and Civil War... on widescreen!

JUDY. Oh, just horrible.

MANNERS. *(Touchy about outside criticism.)* But it had something, wasn't the worst... I twisted myself out of shape to build this guy's part. It was really a sympathetic character.

SHELDON. Sure, everybody was sorry for me.

MANNERS. *(To* **JOHN.***)* Hear you went to college. You're so modest you need a press agent.

SHELDON. He was one of the children in the last revival of *Porgy and Bess*.

MANNERS. Ohhhh, yes...nice clean job.

JUDY. I'm not modest. I finished the Yale drama course. Girls...girls...can go to the Yale drama...

MANNERS. Yale. I'm impressed.

JUDY. You're teasing.

MANNERS. No, you are. Well, where are we? Bill O'Wray is out until tomorrow, he's in a rehearsal for a TV show tonight.

(Proper sighs of regret from the **CAST.***)*

WILETTA. Oh, I was lookin' forward to seein' him today.

SHELDON. Yeah, yeah, nice fella.

MANNERS. Works all the time. *(Now some attention for* **MILLIE.***)* You look gorgeous. This gal has such a flair for clothes. How do you do it?

*(**MILLIE** is pleased. **MANNERS** changes the subject.)*

Ted Bronson is one of our finest writers.

WILETTA. Knows art, knows it.

EDDIE. He was up for an award.

MANNERS. Really, Eddie. I wish you'd let me tell it.

EDDIE. I'm sorry.

MANNERS. Ted's been out on the coast batting out commercial stuff...meat grinder...he's in Europe now... Italy...about a week before he can get back...he did this *Chaos in Belleville* a while back. Producers gave him nothing but howls... "It's ahead of the times!" "Why stick your neck out?" "Why you?"

SHELDON. *(Raises his hand, speaks after **MANNERS** gives him a nod.)* Who is chaos?

EDDIE. Oh, no.

JOHN. *Who?*

MANNERS. *(Holds up his hand for silence.)* Chaos means er...ah, confusion. *Confusion in Belleville*, confusion in a small town.

SHELDON. Ohhhhhh.

MANNERS. I was casually talking to Ted about the er...er, race situation, kicking a few things around...dynamic subject, hard to come to grips with on the screen, TV, anywhere...explosive subject. Suddenly he reaches to the bottom shelf and comes up with *Chaos*. I flipped a few pages...when I read it, bells rang. This is *now*, we're living this, who's in the headlines these days?

(Eloquent pause.)

SHELDON. How 'bout that Montgomery, Alabama? Made the bus company lose one, cold, cash, billion dollars!

JOHN. Not a billion.

MANNERS. Here was a contribution to the elimination of...

SHELDON. I know what I read!

MANNERS. A story of Negro rights that...

SHELDON. How 'bout them buses!

JUDY. And they're absolutely right.

MILLIE. Who's right?

MANNERS. A contribution that really...

JUDY. The colored people.

MANNERS. Leads to a clearer understanding...

MILLIE. Oh, I thought you meant the other people.

MANNERS. A clearer understanding.

JUDY. I didn't mean that.

MANNERS. Yale, please!

> *(All silent.)*

I placed an option on this script so fast...

> *(**SHELDON** raises his hand.)*

I tied it up, Sheldon, so that no one else could get hold of it. When I showed it to Hoskins...

WILETTA. *(To **SHELDON**.)* The producer. Another nice man.

MANNERS. Well, the rest is history. This is my first Broadway show...

> *(Applause from the **CAST**.)*

But I definitely know what I want and however unorthodox my methods, I promise never to bore you.

SHELDON. *(Popping his fingers rapidly.)* He's like that.

MANNERS. I bring to this a burning desire above and beyond anything I've...well, I'm ready to sweat blood. I want to see you kids drawing pay envelopes for a long time to come and...

> (**SHELDON** *applauds; the* **OTHERS** *join him.* **SHELDON** *aims his remark at* **MILLIE**.)

SHELDON. Listen to the man! Listen.

> (**MANNERS** *holds up his hand for silence.*)

MANNERS. At ease. *(Mainly for* **JOHN** *and* **JUDY**.) I ask this, please forget your old methods of work and go along with me. I'll probably confuse the hell out of you for the first few days, but after that...well, I hope we'll be swingin'. Now, you're all familiar with the story...

WILETTA. Oh, I never had anything affect me so much in all my life.

ALL. *(Ad-lib.)* There was one part... I have a question... Uh-huh... A question...

MANNERS. We will not discuss the parts.

> (**JOHN** *groans in mock agony.*)

JUDY. One little thing.

MANNERS. We will *not* discuss the parts.

> (**EDDIE** *smiles knowingly.*)

We will not read the play down from beginning to end.

SHELDON. *(Popping his fingers.)* There he goes!

MANNERS. We will *not* delve into character backgrounds... not now. Turn to Act I, Scene Two, page fifteen.

> (*The* **ACTORS** *scramble madly for places in scripts.*)

Top of the page. Eddie, you read for O'Wray. Judy! Stand up!

(*JUDY stands hesitantly while* **MANNERS** *toys with a sheet of paper.*)

MANNERS. Walk downstage!

(*JUDY is startled and nervous, she walks upstage. The* **OTHERS** *are eager to correct her, but* **MANNERS** *will not tolerate cast interference. He crumbles the paper, throws it to the floor, takes* JUDY *by the shoulders, and speedily leads her around the stage.*)

Downstage! Center stage! Left center! Right center! Up right! Up left, down center, down right, down left, upstage...DOWNSTAGE!

JUDY. I know, I forgot...

MANNERS. Don't forget again. Take downstage.

(*He notices the paper he threw on the floor.*)

A trashy stage is most distracting.

(*JUDY starts to pick up the paper.*)

Hold your position! Wiletta, pick up the paper!

(*JOHN and* **SHELDON** *start for the paper.*)

I asked Wiletta! (*Catching* **WILETTA***'s eye.*) Well?

WILETTA. (*Shocked into a quick flare of temper.*) Well, hell! I ain't the damn janitor! (*Trying to check her temper.*) I...well, I...shucks...I...damn.

(*Even though* **MANNERS** *was trying to catch them off guard, he didn't expect this.*)

MANNERS. Cut! Cut! It's all over.

(*Everyone is surprised again.*)

What you have just seen is...is...is fine acting.

(He is quite shaken and embarrassed from **WILETTA**'s *action.)*

Actors struggle for weeks to do what you have done perfectly...the first time. You gave me anger, frustration, movement, er...excitement. Your faces were alive! Why? You did what came naturally, you believed... That is the quality I want in your work...the firm texture of truth.

JUDY. Oh, you tricked us.

MILLIE. I didn't know what to think.

JOHN. Tension all over the place.

> *(**WILETTA** is still having a hard time getting herself under control. She fans herself with a pocket handkerchief and tries to muster a weak laugh.)*

WILETTA. Yes indeed.

> *(**MANNERS** gingerly touches **WILETTA** and shivers in mock fear.)*

MANNERS. She plays rough. "Well, hell!" Honey, I love you, believe me.

SHELDON. Oh, she cut up!

> *(**WILETTA** tries to laugh along with them, but it's hard going. From this point on, she watches **MANNERS** with a sharp eye, always cautious and on the lookout.)*

WILETTA. Yes...well, let's don't play that no more.

MANNERS. Top of the page. Judy, you're appealing to your father to allow some of his tenant farmers...

> *(He glances at the script to find the next direction. **SHELDON** leans over and whispers to **WILETTA**.)*

WILETTA. Sharecroppers.

SHELDON. Oh.

MANNERS. …Hold a barn dance. Now! Some of them have been talking about voting.

SHELDON. Trouble.

MANNERS. *(Points first to* **MILLIE**, *then* **WILETTA**.*)* Petunia and Ruby are in your father's study…er…er…

(He consults the script again.)

SHELDON. *(Without consulting the script.)* Cleanin' up. Sure, that's what they're doin'.

MANNERS. Tidying up. Your father is going over his account books, you're there…

SHELDON. *(With admiration.)* Lookin' pretty.

MANNERS. There's an awful echo coming from our assistant director.

SHELDON. *(Laughs.)* 'Sistant director! This man breaks me up all the time!

MANNERS. *(Liking the salve.)* What, what did you say?

SHELDON. Say you tickle me to death.

WILETTA. Tickles me too.

MANNERS. Take it!

JUDY. *(Reading.)* Papa, it's a good year, isn't it?

EDDIE. *(With a too-broad Southern accent.)* I'd say fair, fair to middlin'.

(The **CAST** *snickers.)*

MANNERS. All right, Barrymore, just read it.

JUDY. Papa, it's Petunia's birthday today.

EDDIE. That so? Happy birthday, Petunia.

MILLIE. *(Wearily.)* Thank you, sir.

MANNERS. *(Correcting the reading.)* You feel good, full of ginger...your birthday!

MILLIE. *(Remembers the old, standard formula; gives the line with a chuckle and extra warmth.)* Thank you, sir.

JUDY. It would be nice if they could have a stomp in the barn.

MILLIE. *(Her attitude suggesting that* **JUDY** *thought up the line.)* Hmmph.

EDDIE. No need to have any barn stomp until this election business is over.

MILLIE. What the hell is a stomp?

JUDY. I can't see why.

MANNERS. A barn dance. You know that, Millie.

EDDIE. Ruby, you think y'all oughta use the barn?

WILETTA. *(Pleasantly.)* Lord, have mercy, Mr. Renard, don't ask me 'cause I don't know nothin'.

EDDIE. Well, better forget about it.

JUDY. Oh, Papa, let the...let the...

MILLIE. *(For* **JUDY***'s benefit.)* Mmmmmmmmmmph. Why didn't they call it a barn dance?

JUDY. ...Let the... *(Stops reading.)* Oh, must I say that word?

MANNERS. What word?

MILLIE. *Darkies.* That's the word. It says, "Papa, let the darkies have their fun."

MANNERS. *What* do yous want to say?

MILLIE. She could say..."Let *them* have their fun."

MANNERS. But that's Carrie. *(To* **SHELDON.***)* Do you object?

SHELDON. Well, no, not if that's how they spoke in them days.

MANNERS. The time is now, down south in some remote little county, they say those things...now. Can you object in an artistic sense?

SHELDON. No, but you better ask him, he's more artistic than I am.

JOHN. No, I don't object. I don't like the word but it is used, it's a slice of life. Let's face it, Judy wouldn't use it, Mr. Manners wouldn't...

MANNERS. *(Very pleased with **JOHN**'s answer.)* Call me Al, everybody. Al's good enough, Johnny.

JOHN. Al wouldn't say it but Carrie would.

>   *(**MANNERS** gives **WILETTA** an inquiring look.)*

WILETTA. Lord, have mercy, don't ask me 'cause I don't know...

> *(She stops short as she realizes that she is repeating words from the script. She's disturbed that she's repeating the exact line the author indicated. **MANNERS** gives **JUDY** a light tap on the head.)*

MANNERS. Yale! Proceed.

EDDIE. *(Reads.)* Ruby and Petunia leave the room and wait on the porch.

JUDY. Please, Papa, I gave my word. I ask one little thing and...

EDDIE. All right! Before you know it, them niggers will be runnin' me!

JUDY. Please don't use that word!

MANNERS. Oh, stop it!

WILETTA. That's her line in the play, Mr. Manners, Carrie says...

CAST. Please, don't use the word.

*(**MANNERS** signals **EDDIE** to carry on.)*

EDDIE. *(Reads.)* Carrie runs out to the porch.

JUDY. You can use the barn!

MILLIE. Lord, have mercy...

EDDIE. *(Intones.)* Wrong line.

MILLIE. *(Quickly corrects line.)* Er...er, somethin' seems to trouble my spirit, a troublous feelin' is in old Petunia's breast. *(Stops reading.) Old* Petunia?

WILETTA. Yes, *old* Petunia!

JUDY. *(Reads.)* I'm going upstairs to lay out my white organdy dress.

WILETTA. No, you ain't, I'm gonna do that for you.

JUDY. Then I'll take a nap.

MILLIE. No, you ain't, I'm gonna do that for you.

EDDIE. Wrong line.

MILLIE. Sorry. *(Corrects line.)* Yes, child, you rest yourself, you had a terrible hard day. Bless your soul, you just one of God's golden-haired angels.

> *(**MANNERS** is frantically searching for that certain quality. He thinks everything will open once they hit the right chord.)*

MANNERS. Cut! Top of page three, Act I, as it's written. Ruby is shelling beans on the back porch as her son Job approaches.

JOHN. If I can read over...

MANNERS. Do as I ask, do it. Take it, Wiletta.

SHELDON. *(Popping his fingers.)* He's just like that.

WILETTA. *(Reads.)* Boy, where you goin'?

JOHN. Down to Turner's Corner.

WILETTA. You ain't lost nothin' down there. Turner and his brother is talkin' 'bout votin'. I know.

JOHN. They only talkin', I'm goin'.

SHELDON. Mr. Renard say to stay outta that.

JOHN. I got a letter from the president 'bout goin' in the army, Turner says when that happens, a man's s'posed to vote and things.

> **(MILLIE** *and* **JUDY** *are very pleased about this line.)*

SHELDON. Letter ain't from no president, it come from the crackers on the draft board.

JOHN. It *say* from the president.

WILETTA. Pa say you don't go.

> **(MANNERS** *is jotting down a flood of notes.)*

JOHN. Sorry, but I say I'd be there.

SHELDON. I don't know who that boy take after.

EDDIE. Ruby dashes from the porch and Sam follows her. Carrie comes outside and Renard follows her.

> **(EDDIE** *reads Renard.)*

You pamper them rascals too much, see how they do? None of 'em's worth their weight in salt, that boy would steal the egg out of a cake.

> **(JUDY** *tries to laugh, while* **MILLIE** *watches coldly.* **MANNERS** *is amazed at the facial distortion.)*

JUDY. It says laugh.

MANNERS. Well?

JUDY. *(Laughs and continues reading.)* But I can't help feeling sorry for them, they didn't ask to be born.

MILLIE. *(Just loud enough for* **JUDY**'s *ears.)* Hmmmmmmph.

JUDY. I keep thinking, there but for the grace of God go I. If we're superior we should prove it by our actions.

SHELDON. *(Commenting on the line.)* There you go, prove it!

> *(***MANNERS*** is taking more notes. ***JUDY*** is disturbed by the reactions to her reading. She hesitates. ***MANNERS*** looks up. The phone rings. ***EDDIE*** goes off to answer.)*

JUDY. She *is* their friend, right? It's just that I feel reactions and...

MANNERS. What reactions?

MILLIE. I was reacting.

MANNERS. Ohhhhh, who pays Millie any attention, that's her way.

MILLIE. There you go.

SHELDON. Sure is.

JUDY. *(Tries again, but she's very uncomfortable.)* I...I keep thinking...there but for the grace of God...

MANNERS. Are you planning to cry?

JUDY. No, but...no.

> *(She's fighting to hold back the tears.)*

SHELDON. Millie's pickin' on her.

MANNERS. Utter nonsense!

JUDY. My part seems...she seems so smug.

MILLIE. *(To* **SHELDON.***)* Keep my name out of your mouth.

WILETTA. *(To* **SHELDON.***)* Mind your business, your own affairs.

MANNERS. This is fantastic. What in the hell is smug?

> (**HENRY** *enters with a cardboard box full of coffee containers and a large paper bag.*)

Cut! Coffee break! *(To* **JUDY.***)* Especially you.

HENRY. Told the waiter feller to fix up everything nice.

MANNERS. *(Looks in bag.)* What's this?

HENRY. That's what you said. I heard you. "Jelly doughnuts!" you said.

> (**SHELDON** *gets a container of coffee for* **JUDY** *and one for himself.*)

MANNERS. I won't eat it!

HENRY. But I heard you.

MANNERS. Take your coffee and leave.

> (**HENRY** *starts to leave without the coffee.*)

Don't play games, take it with you.

> (**HENRY** *snatches a container and leaves in a quiet huff.* **SHELDON** *hands coffee to* **JUDY,** *but* **MILLIE** *snatches it from his hand.*)

MILLIE. I know you brought that for me.

MANNERS. Where do they find these characters? All right, he's old but it's an imposition…he's probably ninety, you know.

WILETTA. *(Laughs and then suddenly stops.)* We all get old sometimes.

> (**EDDIE** *hurries onstage; looks worried.*)

EDDIE. It's Mrs. Manners...she...she says it's urgent. She has to talk to you *now*...immediately.

MANNERS. Oh, you stupid jerk. Why did you say I was here? You and your big, stupid mouth. Couldn't you say, "He isn't here now, I'll give him your message"?

EDDIE. I'm sorry. She was so...so... Well, she said right off, "I *know* he's there." If I had any idea that she would...

MANNERS. I don't expect you to have *ideas*! Only common sense, just a little common sense. Where do you find a stage manager these days?

EDDIE. I can tell her you can't be disturbed now.

MANNERS. No, numbskull, don't do another thing, you've done enough. *(With wry humor.)* Alimony is not enough, every time I make three extra dollars she takes me to court to get two-thirds of it. If I don't talk to her I'll have a subpoena. You're stupid.

> *(He exits to the telephone. During the brief silence that follows,* **EDDIE** *is miserably self-conscious.)*

WILETTA. *(Tries to save the day.)* Well...I'm glad it's getting a little like winter now. We sure had a hot summer. Did you have a nice summer?

EDDIE. *(Choking back his suppressed anger.)* I worked in stock...summer theater. It was okay.

WILETTA. That's nice. What did you do?

EDDIE. *(Relaxing more.)* Kind of jack-of-all-trades... understudied some, stage-managed, made sets...

MILLIE. And did three people out of a job.

JUDY. I spent the summer with my folks. Soon as we open, I want everyone to come up to Bridgeport and have a glorious day!

(MANNERS returns, looks up briefly.)

JUDY. Daddy makes the yummiest barbecue, you'll love it.

WILETTA. You better discuss it with your folks first.

JUDY. Why?

MILLIE. 'Cause we wouldn't want it discussed after we got there.

SHELDON. No, thank you, ma'am. I'm plannin' to be busy all winter lookin' for an apartment, I sure hate roomin'.

EDDIE. I have my own apartment. It's only a cold-water walk-up but I have it fixed real nice like the magazines show you...whitewashed brick and mobiles hanging in the kitchen and living room. I painted the floors black and spattered them with red and white paint... I learned that in stock...then I shellacked over it and waxed it...and I scraped all of the furniture down to the natural wood...

MILLIE. Oh, hush, you're making me tired. Cold-water flat!

EDDIE. It gives a cheery effect...

MILLIE. And it'll give you double pneumonia.

SHELDON. Yeah, that's the stuff you got to watch.

EDDIE. Well, it's only thirty dollars a month.

SHELDON. They got any colored livin' in that buildin'?

EDDIE. I...I...I don't know. I haven't seen any.

SHELDON. Well, there's none there then.

EDDIE. *(Slightly ill at ease.)* Sheldon, I'll gladly ask.

SHELDON. *(In great alarm.)* Oh, no, no, no! I don't want to be the first.

MILLIE. Damn cold-water flats! I like ease, comfort, furs, cards, big, thick steaks. I want everything.

EDDIE. *(Trying to change the subject.)* Aren't there a lot of new shows this season?

JUDY. My mother says...gosh, every time I open my mouth it's something about my parents. It's not stylish to love your parents...you either have a mother-complex or a father-fixation!

> *(She laughs, and* **MANNERS** *looks up again. He doesn't care for her remarks.)*

But I'm crazy about my parents, but then maybe that's abnormal. I probably have a mother-father-fixation.

WILETTA. What did your mother say?

JUDY. "Never have limitations on your horizon, reach for infinity!" She also feels that everyone has a right to an equal education and not separate either.

JOHN. She sounds like a wonderful woman who...

JUDY. *(Raising her voice.)* Oh, I get so mad about this prejudice nonsense! It's a wonder colored people don't go out and *kill* somebody, I mean actually, really do it... bloody murder, you know?

SHELDON. There's lotsa folks worse off than we are, Millie.

MILLIE. Well, all I hope is that they don't like it, don'tcha know.

MANNERS. *(Boastful about his trials and troubles.)* The seven-year-old kid, the seven-year-old kid...to hear her tell it, our son is ragged, barefoot, hungry...and his teeth are lousy. The orthodontist says he needs braces...they wanta remake his mouth. The kid is falling to pieces. When I go for visitation...he looks in my pockets before he says hello. Can you imagine? Seven years old. The orthodontist and the psychiatrist...the story of my life. But he's a bright kid...smart as a whip...you can't fool him. *(A big sigh.)* Oh, well, let's go. Suppose you were all strangers, had never heard anything about this story except the snatches you heard today. What would you know?

MILLIE. It's my birthday.

>(**WILETTA** *is following him closely; she doesn't care to be caught off guard again.*)

JOHN. Carrie's father has tenant farmers working for him.

MANNERS. Yes and...

JUDY. They want to hold a barn dance and he's against it because...

JOHN. Some of the Negroes are planning to vote for the first time and there's opposition...

SHELDON. His ma and pa don't want him mixed in it 'cause they smell trouble.

JUDY. And my father overheard that John is in it.

SHELDON. And *he don't like it*, that's another thing.

WILETTA. *(Amazed that they have learned so much.)* Mmmmmmm, all of that.

JOHN. But Job is determined.

JUDY. And he's been notified by the draft board.

SHELDON. And the paper, the paper!

MANNERS. Paper?

WILETTA. You know, upstage, downstage, and doin' what comes natural.

MANNERS. Not bad for an hour's work.

EDDIE. Amazing.

SHELDON. *(Popping his fingers.)* Man is on the ball. Fast.

MANNERS. Now we can see how we're heading for the lynching.

SHELDON. *(Starts to peep at back page of script.)* Lynchin'?

MANNERS. We're dealing with an anti-lynch theme. I want it uncluttered, clear in your mind, you must see the skeleton framework within which we're working. Wiletta, turn to the last page of Act I.

EDDIE. Fifty.

MANNERS. Wiletta, dear heart...the end of the act finds you alone on the porch, worried, heartsick...

WILETTA. And singin' a song, sittin', worryin', and singin'.

MANNERS. It's not simply a song, it's a summing up. You're thinking of Renard, the threats, the people and your son...

> (**WILETTA** *is tensely listening, trying to follow him.* **MANNERS** *stands behind her and gently shakes her shoulders.*)

Loosen up, let the thoughts flood over you. I know you have to read...

WILETTA. Oh, I know the song, learned it when I was a child.

MANNERS. Hold a thought, close your eyes, and think aloud...get a good start and then sing...speak your mind and then sing.

WILETTA. *(Not for thinking out loud.)* I know exactly what you want.

MANNERS. Blurt out the first thing that enters your mind.

WILETTA. *(Sings a mournful dirge of despair.)*
COME AND GO WITH ME TO THAT LAND,
COME AND GO WITH ME TO THAT LAND...

MANNERS. Gosh, that guy can write.

WILETTA.
COME AND GO WITH ME TO THAT LAND WHERE I'M
BOUND

NO CONFUSION IN THAT LAND,
NO CONFUSION IN THAT LAND
NO CONFUSION IN THAT LAND WHERE I'M BOUND...

MILLIE. *(Wipes her eyes.)* A heartbreaker.

EDDIE. Oh, Wiletta, it's so...so...gosh.

JOHN. Leaves you weak.

MANNERS. Beautiful. What were you thinking?

WILETTA. *(Ready to move on to something else.)* Thank you.

MANNERS. What were you thinking?

WILETTA. I thought...I...er, er... I don't know, whatever you said.

MANNERS. Tell me. You're not a vacuum, you thought something.

JOHN. Your motivation. What motivated...

MANNERS. *(Waving* **JOHN** *out of it.)* You thought *something*, right?

WILETTA. Uh-huh.

MANNERS. And out of the thought came song.

WILETTA. Yeah.

MANNERS. What did you think?

WILETTA. I thought that's what you wanted.

> *(She realizes she is the center of attention and finds it uncomfortable.)*

MANNERS. It won't do. You must know why you do a thing, that way you're true to me, to the part, and yourself...

WILETTA. Didn't you like it?

MANNERS. Very much but...I'm sure you've never worked this way before, but you're not carrying a tray or answering doorbells, this is substance, meat. I demand that you *know* what you're doing and *why*, at all times, I will accept nothing less.

WILETTA. *(To* **JOHN** *and* **JUDY.***)* I know, you have to justify.

SHELDON. *(Worried and trying to help* **WILETTA.***)* You was thinkin' how sad it was, wasn't you?

WILETTA. Uh-huh.

MANNERS. It's new to you but it must be done. Let go, think aloud and when you are moved to do so...sing.

> *(***WILETTA** *looks blank.)*

Start anywhere.

WILETTA. Ah, er...it's so sad that folks can't vote...it's also sad that er, er...

MANNERS. No.

> *(He picks up the newspaper.)*

We'll try word association. I'll give you a word, then you say what comes to your mind and keep on going... one word brings on another... Montgomery!

WILETTA. Alabama.

MANNERS. Montgomery!

WILETTA. Alabama.

MANNERS. Montgomery!

WILETTA. Reverend King is speakin' on Sunday.

MANNERS. Colored.

WILETTA. Lights changin' colors all around me.

MANNERS. Colored.

WILETTA. They...they...

MANNERS. Colored.

WILETTA. "They got any colored in that buildin'?"

MANNERS. Children, little children.

WILETTA. Children...children... "Pick up that paper!" Oh, my...

MANNERS. Lynching.

WILETTA. Killin'! Killin'!

MANNERS. Killing.

WILETTA. It's the man's theater, the man's money, so what you gonna do?

MANNERS. Oh, Wiletta... I don't know! *Darkness!*

WILETTA. A star! Oh, I can't, I don't like it...

MANNERS. Sing.

WILETTA. *(Sings a song of strength and anger.)*
COME AND GO WITH ME TO THAT LAND

> *(The song is overpowering; we see a woman who could fight the world.)*

COME AND GO WITH ME TO THAT LAND
COME AND GO WITH ME TO THAT LAND –
WHERE I'M BOUND.

JUDY. Bravo! Magnificent!

MANNERS. Wiletta, if you dare! You will undo us! Are you out of your senses? When you didn't know what you were doing...perfection on the nose. I'll grant you the first interpretation was right, without motivating. All right, I'll settle for that.

WILETTA. *(Feeling very lost.)* I said I *knew* what you wanted.

MANNERS. Judy! I...I want to talk to you about...about Carrie.

> *(He rises and starts for the dressing room.)*

Eddie, will you dash out and get me a piece of danish? Okay, at ease.

(**EDDIE** *quickly exits.* **MANNERS** *and* **JUDY** *exit stage right toward the dressing rooms.*)

MILLIE. *(To* **JOHN.***)* Look, don't get too close to her.

SHELDON. Mind your own business.

JOHN. What have I done?

MILLIE. You're too friendly with her.

WILETTA. Justify. Ain't enough to do it, you got to justify.

JOHN. I've only been civil.

MILLIE. That's too friendly.

WILETTA. Got a splittin' headache.

SHELDON. *(To* **WILETTA.***)* I wish I had an aspirin for you.

MILLIE. *(To* **JOHN.***)* All set to run up and see her folks. Didn't you hear her say they expect something terrible to happen to her? Well, you're one of the terrible things they have in mind!

SHELDON. Mind your business.

MILLIE. It is my business. When they start raisin' a fund for his defense, they're gonna come and ask me for money and I'll have to be writin' the president and signin' petitions…so it's my business.

SHELDON. I tell you, son. I'm friendly with white folks in a distant sorta way but I don't get too close. Take Egypt, Russia, all these countries, why they kickin' up their heels? 'Cause of white folks, I wouldn't trust one of 'em sittin' in front of me on a merry-go-round, wouldn't trust 'em if they was laid up in bed with lockjaw and the mumps both at the same time.

JOHN. Last time I heard from you, you said it was the colored who made all the trouble.

SHELDON. They do, they're the worst ones. There's two kinda people that's got the world messed up for good, that's the colored and the white, and I got no use for either one of 'em.

MILLIE. I'm going to stop trying to help people.

JOHN. Hell, I'm through with it. Oh, I'm learning the ropes!

SHELDON. *That's* why they don't do more colored shows... troublemakers, potboilers, spoon stirrers...and sharper than a serpent's tooth! Colored women wake up in the mornin' with their fists ball up...ready to fight.

WILETTA. What in the devil is all this justifyin'? Ain't necessary.

MILLIE. *(To* **SHELDON.***)* And you crawlin' all over me to hand her coffee! Damn "Tom."

SHELDON. You talkin' 'bout your relatives, ain't talkin' 'bout me, if I'm a "Tom," you a "Jemima."

JOHN. I need out, I need air.

(He exits stage left.)

SHELDON. White folks is stickin' together, stickin' together, stickin' together...we fightin'.

WILETTA. Hush, I got a headache.

MILLIE. I need a breath of air, too, before I slap the taste out of somebody's mouth.

(She grabs her coat and exits stage left.)

SHELDON. I hope the wind blows her away. They gonna kick us until we all out in the street...unemployed... get all the air you want then. Sometimes I take low, yes, gotta take low. Man says somethin' to me, I say... "Yes, sure, certainly." You 'n' me know how to do. That ain't *Tommin'*, that's common sense. You and me...we don't mind takin' low because we tryin' to accomplish somethin'...

WILETTA. I mind... I do mind... I mind... I mind...

SHELDON. Well, yeah, we all mind...but you got to swaller what you mind. What you mind won't buy beans. I mean, you gotta take what you mind to survive...to eat, to breathe...

WILETTA. *(Tensely.) I mind.* Leave me alone.

> (**SHELDON** *exits with a sigh.* **HENRY** *enters, carrying a lunch box.* **WILETTA** *turns; she looks so distressed.)*

HENRY. They've all flown the coop?

WILETTA. Yes.

HENRY. What's the matter? Somebody hurt your feelin's?

WILETTA. Yes.

HENRY. Don't fret, it's too nice a day. I believe in treatin' folks right. When you're just about through with this life, that's the time when you know how to live. Seems like yesterday I was forty years old and the day before that I wasn't but nineteen... Think of it.

WILETTA. I don't like to think...makes me fightin' mad.

HENRY. *(Giving vent to his pent-up feelings.)* Don't I know it? When he yelled about jelly doughnuts, I started to land one on him! Oh, I almost did it!

WILETTA. I know it!

HENRY. But... "Hold your temper!" I says. I have a most ferocious temper.

WILETTA. Me too. I take and take, then watch out!

HENRY. Have to hold my temper, I don't want to kill the man.

WILETTA. Yeah, makes you feel like fightin'.

HENRY. *(Joining in the spirit of the discussion.)* Sure I'm a fighter and I come from a fightin' people.

WILETTA. You from Ireland?

HENRY. A fightin' people! Didn't we fight for the home rule?

WILETTA. Uh-huh, now you see there.

> (**WILETTA** *doesn't worry about making sense out of* **HENRY***'s speech on Ireland; it's the feeling behind it that counts.*)

HENRY. Oh, a history of great men, fightin' men!

WILETTA. *(Rallying to the call, she answers as though sitting on an amen bench at a revival meeting.)* Yes, carry on.

HENRY. Ah, yes, we was fightin' for the home rule! Ah, there was some great men!

WILETTA. I know it.

HENRY. There was Parnell! Charles Stewart Parnell!

WILETTA. All right!

HENRY. A figure of a man! The highest! Fightin' hard for the home rule! A parliamentarian! And they clapped him in the blasted jailhouse for six months!

WILETTA. Yes, my lord!

HENRY. And Gladstone introduced the bill...and later on you had Dillon and John Redmond...and then when the home rule was almost put through, what did you think happened? World War I! That killed the whole business!

WILETTA. *(Very indignant.)* Oh, if it ain't one thing, it's another!

HENRY. I'm descended from a great line! And then the likes of him with his jelly doughnuts! Jelly doughnuts, indeed, is it? What does he know? Tramplin' upon a man's dignity! Me father was the greatest, most dignified man you've ever seen...and he played vaudeville! Oh, the bearin' of him! *(Angrily demonstrating his father's* *dignity.)* Doin' the little soft-shoe step...and it's take your hat off to the ladies...and step along there...

WILETTA.   Henry, I want to be an actress. I've always wanted to be an actress and they ain't gonna do me the way they did the home rule! I want to be an actress 'cause one day you're nineteen and then forty and so on... I want to be an actress! Henry, they stone us when we try to go to school, the world's crazy.

HENRY.   It's a shame, a shame...

WILETTA.   Where the hell do I come in? Every damn body pushin' me off the face of the earth! I want to be an actress...hell, I'm gonna be one, you hear me?

(She pounds the table.)

HENRY.   Sure, and why not, I'd like to know!

WILETTA.   *(Quietly.)* Yes, dammit...and why not? Why in the hell not?

(Blues record in; woman singer.*)

---

*A license to produce *Trouble in Mind* does not include a performance license for any third-party or copyrighted music. Licensees should create an original composition or use music in the public domain. For further information, please see the Music and Third-Party Materials Use Note on page iii.

ACT II

(The theater. Ten o'clock Thursday morning. Blues music in, up, and out.* Furniture has been changed around; some of the old set removed. BILL O'WRAY, a character actor [white], stands upstage on a makeshift platform. He radiates strength and power as he addresses an imaginary audience. MANNERS stands stage left, tie loosened, hair ruffled. He is hepped up with nervous energy, can barely stand still. EDDIE is stage right, in charge of the script and a tape recorder; he follows the script and turns up the tape recorder on cue from MANNERS. BILL is delivering a "masterful" rendition of Renard's speech on "tolerance." MANNERS is elated one moment, deflated the next. EDDIE is obviously nervous, drawn, and lacking the easygoing attitude of Act I.)

BILL. *(Intones speech with vigor and heartfelt passion.)* My friends, if all the world were just, there would be no need for valor... And those of us who are of a moderate mind... I would say the majority... *(Light applause from tape recorder.)* ...we are anything but lighthearted. But the moving finger writes and having writ moves *on.* No you can't wash out a word of it. Heretofore we've gotten along with our Nigra population...but times change.

---

*A license to produce *Trouble in Mind* does not include a performance license for any third-party or copyrighted music. Licensees should create an original composition or use music in the public domain. For further information, please see the Music and Third-Party Materials Use Note on page iii.

BILL. *(Applause from tape recorder.)* I do not argue with any man who believes in segregation. I, of all people, will not, cannot question that belief. We all believe in the words of Henry Clay: "Sir, I would rather be right than be president."

(**EDDIE** *sleeps his cue.*)

MANNERS. Dammit! Eddie!

(**EDDIE** *suddenly switches to loud applause.*)

BILL. But difficulties are things that show what men are, and necessity is still the mother of invention. As Emerson so aptly pointed out: "The true test of civilization is not the – census, nor the size of cities, nor the crops – but the kind of man the country turns out." Oh, my friends, let every man look before he leaps, let us consider submitting to the present evil lest a greater one befall us – say to yourself, my honor is dearer to me than my life. *(Very light applause.)* I say moderation – for these are the times that try men's souls! In these terrible days we must realize – how oft the darkest hour of ill breaks brightest into dawn. Moderation, yes. *(Very light applause.)* Even the misguided, infamous Adolph Hitler said: "One should guard against believing the great masses to be more stupid than they actually are!" *(Applause.)* Oh, friends, moderation. Let us weigh our answer very carefully when the dark-skinned Oliver Twist approaches our common pot and says: "Please, sir, I want some more." When we say: "No," remember that a soft answer turneth away wrath. Ohhh, we shall come out of the darkness, and sweet is pleasure after pain. If we are superior, let us show our superiority!

(**MANNERS** *directs* **EDDIE** *to take applause up high and then out.*)

Moderation. With wisdom and moderation, these terrible days will pass. I am reminded of the immortal words of Longfellow:

And the night shall be filled with music,
And the cares, that infest the day,
Shall fold their tents, like the Arabs,
And as silently steal away.

> *(Terrific applause. **MANNERS** slaps **BILL** on his back, dashes to **EDDIE**, and turns the applause up and down.)*

MANNERS. Is this such a Herculean task? All you have to do is listen! Inattention – aggravates the hell out of me!

> *(When **BILL** drops out of character, we see that he is very different from the strong Renard. He appears to be worried at all times. He has a habit of negatively shaking his head even though nothing is wrong. **BILL O'WRAY** is but a shadow of a man – but by some miracle he turns into a dynamic figure as Renard. As **BILL** – he sees dragons in every corner and worries about each one.)*

BILL. I don't know, I don't know...

> *(**MANNERS** fears the worst for the show as he watches **BILL**.)*

MANNERS. What? What is it?

BILL. *(Half-dismissing the thought.)* Oh, well... I guess...

> *(**EDDIE** is toying with the machine and turns the applause up by accident.)*

MANNERS. Hello, Eddie, a little consideration! Why do you do it? Damned childish!

> *(**EDDIE** turns off the machine.)*

What's bothering you?

BILL. Well, you never can tell...but I don't know...

MANNERS. Bill, cut it out, come on.

BILL. That Arab stuff...you know, quietly folding his tent...you're gonna get a laugh...and then on the other hand you might offend somebody...well, we'll see...

MANNERS. Eddie, make a note of that. Arab folding his tent. I'll take it up with Bronson.

    (**EDDIE** *is making notes.*)

BILL. I'm tellin' you, you don't need it...wouldn't lose a thing...the Longfellow quote... I don't know, maybe I'm wrong but...

MANNERS. You act like you've lost your last friend! I'm the one holding the blasted bag!

    (**BILL** *takes* Show Business Weekly *out of his coat pocket.*)

BILL. Well, maybe I shouldn't have said...

MANNERS. I'm out of my mind! When I think of the money borrowed and for what! Oh, I'm just talking. This always happens when the ship leaves port. The union's making me take three extra stagehands... *(Laughs.)* They hate *us*! Co-produce, filthy word! You know who I had to put the bite on for an extra ten thousand? My ex-wife's present boyfriend. Enough to emasculate a man for the rest of his life!

BILL. How is Fay? Sweet kid. I was sure surprised when you two broke it off. Oh, well, that's the way...

MANNERS. She's fine and we're good friends. Thank God for civilization.

BILL. That's nice. Ten thousand? She must have connected up with a big wheel, huh?

MANNERS. I've known you long enough to ask a favor.

BILL. All depends.

MANNERS. Will you stop running off at lunch hour? It looks bad.

BILL. Now, wait a minute...

EDDIE. I eat with them all the time.

MANNERS. Drop it, Eddie. Unity in *this* company is very important. Hell, I don't care, but it looks like you don't want to eat with the colored members of the cast.

BILL. I don't.

EDDIE. I guess you heard him.

MANNERS. Bill, this is fantastic. I never credited you with this kind of...silly, childlike...

BILL. There's not a prejudiced bone in my body. It is important that I eat my lunch. I used to have an ulcer. I have nothing against anybody but I can't eat my damn lunch...people *stare*. They sit there glaring and staring.

MANNERS. Nonsense.

BILL. Tuesday I lunched with Millie because I bumped into her on the street. That restaurant...people straining and looking at me as if I were an old lecher! God knows what they're thinking. I've got to eat my lunch. After all... I can't stand that...

MANNERS. *(Laughs.)* All right but mix a little...it's the show...do it for the show.

BILL. Every time I open my mouth somebody is telling me don't say this or that... Millie doesn't want to be called "gal"... I call *all* women "gal"... I don't know... I'm not going into analysis about this... I'm not. How do you think my character is shaping up?

MANNERS. Great, no complaints...fine.

> *(**WILETTA** drags in, tired and worn.)*

Morning, sweetie.

EDDIE. Good morning.

WILETTA. *(Indicating script.)* I been readin' this back and forth and over again.

MANNERS. *(Automatic sympathy.)* Honey, don't...

WILETTA. My neighbor, Miss Green, she come up and held the book and I sat there justifyin' like you said...

MANNERS. Darling, don't think. You're great until you start thinking. I don't expect you to...

WILETTA. *(Weak laugh.)* I've been in this business a long time, more than twenty-five years and...

MANNERS. Don't tell it, you're beautiful.

WILETTA. Guess I can do like the others. We was justifyin' and Miss Green says to me...

BILL. *(Gets in his good deed.)* Wiletta, you look wonderful, you really do.

WILETTA. Huh?

BILL. You...you're looking well.

WILETTA. Thank you, Miss Green says...

MANNERS. *(Wearily.)* Oh, a plague on Miss Green. Darling, it's too early to listen to outside criticism, it can be dangerous if the person doesn't understand...

WILETTA. Miss Green puts on shows at the church...and she had an uncle that was a sharecropper, so she says the first act...

MANNERS. *(Flips the script to Act III.)* We're hitting the third today.

WILETTA. Miss Green also conducts the church choir...

MANNERS. Wiletta, don't complicate my life. *(To BILL and EDDIE.)* Isn't she wonderful? *(To WILETTA.)* Dear heart, I adore you.

WILETTA. *(Feels like a fool as she limply trails on.)* She... she did the *Messiah*... Handel's *Messiah*...last Easter... and folks come from downtown to hear it...all kinds of folks...white folks too.

MANNERS. Eddie! Did I leave the schedule at home?

(EDDIE hands him the schedule.)

EDDIE. I have a copy.

WILETTA. Miss Green says, now...she said it...she says the third act doesn't justify with the first...no, wait... her exact words was, "The third act is not the natural outcome of the first." I thought, I thought she might be right.

MANNERS. *(Teasing.)* Make me a solemn promise, don't start thinking.

(SHELDON enters in a rush and hastily begins to remove scarves, coat, etc.)

SHELDON. Good mornin', there ain't no justice.

(BILL glances at Show Business from time to time.)

EDDIE. What a greeting.

SHELDON. I dreamed six, twelve, six, one, two...just like that. You know what come out yesterday? Six, one, three. What you gonna do?

MANNERS. Save your money.

BILL. Hey, what do you know?

MANNERS. Did we make the press?

SHELDON. *(To WILETTA.)* Friend of mine died yesterday, went to see about his apartment...gone! Just like that!

BILL. Gary Brewer's going into rehearsal on *Lost and Lonely*.

MANNERS. Been a long time.

BILL. He was in that Hollywood investigation some years ago.

SHELDON. *(To* **EDDIE.***)* They musta applied whilst the man was dyin'.

MANNERS. He wasn't really in it, someone named him I think.

BILL. You knew him well, didn't you?

MANNERS. Me? I don't know him. I've worked with him a couple of times but I don't really know him.

BILL. A very strange story reached me once, some fellow was planning to name me, can you imagine?

> *(**MILLIE** enters, wearing a breathtaking black suit. She is radiant.)*

EDDIE. That's ridiculous.

BILL. Nothing ever happened, but that's the story. Naming *me.*

MANNERS. *(As he studies the schedule.)* Talking about the coast, I could be out there now on a honey of a deal... but this I had to do, that's all.

SHELDON. Y'all ever hear my stories 'bout people namin' me?

MANNERS. What?

BILL. Oh, Shel!

> *(This is a burden **SHELDON** has carried for quite some time.)*

SHELDON. I sang on a program once with Millie, to help some boy that was in trouble...but later on I heard they was tryin' to overthrow the gov'ment.

> *(**MANNERS, EDDIE,** and **BILL** are embarrassed by this.)*

MILLIE. Oh, hush! Your mouth runs like a racehorse!

SHELDON. Well, ain't nothin' wrong with singin' is there? We just sang.

MILLIE. *(As she removes her hat.)* A big fool.

MANNERS. *(Making peace.)* Oh, now...we're all good Americans.

BILL. *(To ease the tension.)* I...I...er, didn't know you went in for singing, Sheldon.

SHELDON. Sure, I even wrote me a coupla tunes. Can make a lotta money like that but you gotta know somebody, I ain't got no pull.

WILETTA. *(To* **MILLIE.***)* He talks too much, talks too much.

MANNERS. Ah, we have a composer, popular stuff?

> *(***SHELDON*** stands and mechanically rocks to and fro in a rock-and-roll beat as he sings:)*

SHELDON.
YOU-OO-HOO-OO ARE MY HON-HONEY
OOO-OO-OOO-OO, YOU SMILE IS SU-HU-HUNNY
MY HU-HU-HUNNY, BAY-HAY-HAY-BEE-E-E-E

...And it goes like that.

MANNERS. Well!

SHELDON. Thank you.

BILL. I don't know why you haven't sold it, that's all you hear.

> *(***SHELDON*** is pleased with ***BILL****'s compliment but also a little worried.)*

MILLIE. Hmmmmmph.

EDDIE. Really a tune.

SHELDON. *(To* **BILL.***)* My song...it...it's copyrighted.

BILL. Oh?

SHELDON. I got papers.

MILLIE. *(Extends her wrist to* **WILETTA.***)* Look. My husband is in off the road.

WILETTA. What's the matter?

MILLIE. A new watch, and I got my suit out...brought me this watch. We looked at a freezer this morning...food freezer...what's best, a chest freezer or an upright? I don't know.

> *(***JUDY*** *enters, dressed a little older than in Act I; her hair is set with more precision. She is reaching for a sophistication that can never go deeper than the surface. She often makes graceful, studied postures and tries new attitudes, but very often she forgets.)*

JUDY. Greetings and salutations. Sheldon, how are you, dear?

SHELDON. Thank you.

JUDY. *(As* **MILLIE** *displays her wrist for inspection.)* Millie, darling, how lovely, ohhhhh, exquisite...

WILETTA. *(Really trying to join in.)* Mmmmm, ain't it divine.

> *(***HENRY*** *and* ***JOHN*** *enter together.* ***HENRY*** *carries a container of coffee and a piece of danish for* ***MANNERS.*** ***HENRY*** *is exact, precise, all business. He carries the container to* ***MANNERS****'s table, places pastry, taps* ***EDDIE*** *on the shoulder, points to* ***MANNERS****, points to container, nods to* ***MANNERS*** *and company, turns, and leaves, all while dialogue continues.* ***JOHN*** *enters on a cloud. He is drifting more and more toward the heady heights of opportunism. He sees himself on the brink of escaping* ***WILETTA, MILLIE,*** *and* ***SHELDON.*** *It's becoming very easy to conform to* ***MANNERS****' pattern.)*

JOHN. I'm walking in my sleep. I was up all hours last night.

MANNERS. At Sardi's no doubt.

JOHN. No!

JUDY. Exposed! We've found you out.

> *(General laughter from **MILLIE**, **JUDY**, **BILL**, **EDDIE**, and **MANNERS**. **JUDY** is enjoying the intangible joke to the utmost, but as she turns to **WILETTA**, her laughter dies...but **WILETTA** quickly picks it up.)*

WILETTA. Oh, my, yes indeed!

JOHN. I struggled with the third act. I think I won.

> *(**MILLIE** sticks out her wrist for **JOHN**'s inspection.)*

Exquisite, Millie, beautiful. You deserve it.

> *(During the following, the conversation tumbles criss-cross in all directions, and the only clear things are underlined.)*

MANNERS. Tell him what I told you this morning.

BILL. Why should I swell his head?

MANNERS. *(Arm around **JOHN**'s shoulder.)* <u>Hollywood's going to grab you so fast!</u> I won't drop names but our opening night is going to be the end.

MILLIE. *(To **WILETTA**.)* <u>Barbara died!</u>

JUDY. *(To **MANNERS**.)* Oh, you terrify me!

MILLIE. <u>Died alone in her apartment.</u> Sudden-like!

JOHN. I've got to catch Katherine's performance, I hear it's terrific!

BILL. She's great, only great.

MILLIE. <u>I wouldn't live alone!</u>

MANNERS. She's going to get the award, no doubt about it!

JUDY. Marion Hatterly is good.

MANNERS. Marion is as <u>old as the hills!</u> I mean, she's so old it's embarrassing.

JOHN. But she has a quality.

SHELDON. *(To* **MILLIE** *and* **WILETTA.***)* <u>People dyin' like they got nothin' else to do!</u>

JUDY. She has, John, a real quality.

SHELDON. <u>I ain't gonna die,</u> can't afford to do it.

MANNERS. You have to respect her.

EDDIE. Can name her own ticket.

JOHN. Imperishable talent.

MILLIE. <u>Funeral is Monday.</u>

WILETTA. *(Weakly, to no one in particular.)* Mmmmm, fascinatin'...

MANNERS. Picnic is over! Third act!

SHELDON. I know my lines.

BILL. Don't worry about lines yet.

MANNERS. No, let him worry... I mean it's okay. Beginning of third!

> (**WILETTA** *feels dizzy from past conversation. She rises and walks in a half circle, then half circles back again. She is suddenly the center of attraction.)*

WILETTA. It...it's nighttime and I'm ironin' clothes.

MANNERS. Right. We wander through it. Here's the ironing board, door, window...you iron. Carrie is over there crying.

JUDY. Oh, poor, dear, Carrie, crying again.

MANNERS. Petunia is near the window, looking out for Job. Everyone is worried, worried, worried like crazy. Have the lynchers caught Job? Sam is seated in the corner, whittling a stick.

SHELDON. *(Flat statement.)* Whittlin' a stick.

MANNERS. Excitement. Everyone knows that a mob is gathering.

> (**SHELDON** *is seated and busy running one index finger over the other.*)

SHELDON. I'm whittlin' a stick.

MANNERS. *(Drumming up excitement.)* The hounds can be heard baying in the distance.

> (**SHELDON** *bays to fill in the dog bit.* **MANNERS** *silences him with a gesture.*)

Everyone *listens*! They are thinking – has Job been killed? Ruby begins to sing.

> (**WILETTA** *begins to sing with a little too much power, but* **MANNERS** *directs her down.*)

WILETTA.
> LORD, HAVE MERCY, LORD HAVE MERCY... *(Hums.)*

MILLIE. *(In abject, big-eyed fear.)* Listen to them dogs in the night.

> (**MANNERS** *warns* **SHELDON** *not to provide sound effects.*)

WILETTA. *(Trying to lose herself in the part.)* Child, you better go now.

> (**BILL** *whispers to* **EDDIE.**)

EDDIE. *Line. Miss Carrie*, you better go now.

MANNERS. Oh, bother! Don't do that!

(**EDDIE** *feels resentful toward* **BILL** *as* **BILL**
*acts as though he had nothing to do with the
correction.*)

WILETTA. This ain't no place for you to be.

(**JUDY** *now plays Carrie in a different way
from Act I. There is a reserved kindliness,
rather than real involvement.*)

JUDY. I don't want to leave you alone, Ruby.

SHELDON. Thassa mistake, Mr. Manners. She can't be
alone if me and Millie is there with her.

MANNERS. Don't interrupt!

SHELDON. Sorry.

(**BILL** *shakes his fist at* **SHELDON** *in playful
pantomime.*)

WILETTA. Man that is born of woman is but a few days and
full of trouble.

JUDY. I'm going to drive over to the next county and get
my father and Judge Willis.

MILLIE. No, you ain't. Mr. Renard would never forgive me
if somethin' was to happen to you.

(**SHELDON** *is very touched and sorry for all
concerned as he whittles his stick.*)

JUDY. I feel so helpless.

SHELDON. *(Interrupts out of sheer frustration.)* Am I still
whittlin' the stick?

WILETTA. Dammit, yes.

MANNERS. *(Paces to control his annoyance.)* Shel.

SHELDON. I thought I lost my place.

WILETTA. *(Picks up* **MANNERS'** *signal.)* Nothin' to do now but pray!

SHELDON. *(Recognizes his cue.)* Oh, yeah, that's me. *(Knows his lines almost perfectly.)* Lord, once and again and one more time...

> *(***MILLIE** *moans in the background.* **WILETTA'***s mind seems a thousand miles away.* **MANNERS** *snaps his fingers, and she begins to moan background for* **SHELDON'***s prayer.)*

Your humble servant calls on your everlastin' mercy...

MILLIE. Yes, Lord!

SHELDON. ...To beseech, to beseech thy help for all your children this evenin'...

MILLIE. This evenin', Lord.

> *(***MANNERS** *is busy talking to* **JOHN.***)*

SHELDON. But most of all we ask, we pray...that you help your son and servant Job...

WILETTA. Help him, Lord!

SHELDON. *(Doing a grand job of the prayer.)* Walk with Job! Talk with Job! Ohhhhh, be with Job!

JUDY. Yes!

> *(***MANNERS** *and* **BILL** *give* **JUDY** *disapproving looks, and she clasps her hand over her mouth.)*

WILETTA. *(Starts to sing and is joined by* **SHELDON** *and* **MILLIE.***)*
DEATH AIN'T NOTHIN' BUT A ROBBER, CAN'TCHA SEE, CAN'TCHA SEE...

> *(***MANNERS** *is in a real tizzy, watching to catch* **BILL'***s reaction to the scene, and trying*

with his whole body to keep the scene up and going.)

MANNERS. Eddie! Direction!

EDDIE. The door opens and Job enters!

WILETTA. Job, why you come here?

> (**MANNERS** *doesn't like her reading. It is too direct and thoughtful.)*

MILLIE. *(Lashing out.)* They after you! They told you 'bout mixin' in with Turner and that votin'!

MANNERS. Oh, good girl!

WILETTA. I'm the one to talk to my boy!

JOHN. *(A frightened, shivering figure.)* If somebody could get me a wagon, I'll take the low road around Simpkin's Hollow and catch a train goin' away from here.

WILETTA. Shoulda gone 'fore you started this misery.

> (**MANNERS** *indicates that she should get rougher; she tries.)*

Screamin' 'bout your rights! You got none! You got none!

JOHN. I'm askin' for help, I gotta leave.

MANNERS. *(To **JOHN**.)* Appeal, remember it's an appeal.

JOHN. *(As though a light has dawned.)* Ah, you're so right. *(Reads with tender appeal.)* I gotta leave.

MANNERS. Right.

WILETTA. You tryin' to tell me that you runnin' away?

SHELDON. *(Worried about Job's escape and getting caught up outside of the scene.)* Sure! That's what he said in the line right there!

> (**MANNERS** *silences **SHELDON** with a gesture.)*

WILETTA. You say you ain't done nothin' wrong?

(**MANNERS** *looks at* **EDDIE** *and* **BILL** *with despair.*)

JOHN. I ain't lyin'...

WILETTA. Then there's no need to be runnin'. Ain't you got no faith?

SHELDON. (*Sings in a shaky voice as he raps out time.*)
OH, WELL, A TIME OF TROUBLE IS A LONESOME TIME
TIME OF TROUBLE IS A LONESOME TIME...

(*Joined by* **MILLIE**:)
FEEL LIKE I COULD DIE, FEEL LIKE I COULD DIE...

WILETTA. Tell 'em you sorry, tell 'em you done wrong!

MANNERS. Relate, Wiletta. Relate to what's going on around you! (*To* **JOHN.**) Go on.

JOHN. I wasn't even votin' for a Black man, votin' for somebody white same as they.

(*Aside to* **MANNERS.**) Too much? Too little? I fell off.

(**MANNERS** *indicates that he's on the beam.*)

WILETTA. I ain't never voted!

SHELDON. No, Lord!

WILETTA. I don't care who get in! Don't make no nevermind to us!

MILLIE. The truth?

JOHN. (*All afire.*) When a man got a decent word to say for us down here, I gonna vote for him.

WILETTA. A decent word! And that's all you ever gonna get outta him. Dammit! He ain't gonna win no how! They done said he ain't and they gonna see to it! And you gonna be dead...for a decent word!

JOHN. I ain't gonna wait to be killed.

WILETTA. There's only one right thing to do!

(**CAST** *turns page in unison.*)

You got to go and give yourself up.

JOHN. But I ain't done nothin'.

SHELDON. *(Starts to sing again.)*
WELLA, TROUBLE IS A LONESOME THING... LONESOME...
LONESOME...

MANNERS. *(The song even grates on him.)* Cut it, it's too much.

JUDY. My father will have you put in the county jail where you'll be safe.

JOHN. But I ain't done nothin'!

JUDY. I'm thinking of Ruby and the others, even if you aren't. I don't want murder in this community.

WILETTA. *(Screams.)* Boy, get down on your knees.

MANNERS. *(To* **EDDIE.***)* Muscular tension.

(**EDDIE** *makes a note.*)

WILETTA. Oh, Lord, touch this boy's heart!

SHELDON. Mmmmmm, hmmmmmmm. Hmmmmmmm...

WILETTA. Reach him tonight! Take the fear and hatred out of his soul!

MILLIE. Mercy, Lord!

JOHN. Stop, I can't stand no more. Whatever you say, anything you say.

SHELDON. Praise the Lord!

EDDIE. Renard enters.

BILL. Carrie, you shouldn't be here.

WILETTA. I told her. I'm beggin' you to help my boy, sir...

(She drops the script and picks it up.)

JOHN. Ohhh, I can't sustain.

MANNERS. Don't try. We're breaking everything down to the simplest components... I want simple reactions to given circumstances in order to highlight the outstanding phases.

*(***WILETTA*** finds her place.)*

Okay, let it roll.

WILETTA. I'm beggin' you to help my boy.

BILL. Boy, you're a mighty little fella to fly in the face of things people live by 'round here. I'll do what I can, what little I can.

WILETTA. Thank you, sir.

JUDY. Have Judge Willis put him in jail where he'll be safe.

BILL. Guess it wasn't his fault.

WILETTA. He don' know nothin'.

BILL. There are all kinds of white men in the world.

SHELDON. The truth.

BILL. This bird Akins got to sayin' the kind of things that was bound to stir you folks up.

MILLIE. I ain't paid him no mind myself.

BILL. Well, anything you want to take to the jailhouse with you? Like a washcloth and...well, whatever you might need.

JOHN. I don't know, don't know what I'm doin'.

BILL. Think you learned a lesson from all this?

MILLIE. You hear Mr. Renard?

SHELDON. He wanna know if you learned your lesson.

JOHN. I believed I was right.

SHELDON. Now you know you wasn't.

BILL. If anything happens, you tell the men Mr. Akins put notions in your head, understand?

SHELDON. He wanna know if you understand.

BILL. Come along, we'll put you in the jailhouse. Reckon I owe your ma and pa that much.

JOHN. I'm afraid, I so afraid...

MILLIE. Just go, 'fore they get here.

EDDIE. Job turns and looks at his father.

> (**SHELDON** *places one finger to his lips and throws up his arms to show that he has no line.*)

Finally, he looks to his mother, she goes back to her ironing.

BILL. Petunia, see that Miss Carrie gets home safe.

MILLIE. Yes, sir.

EDDIE. Job follows Renard out into the night as Ruby starts to sing.

WILETTA.
KEEP ME FROM SINKIN' DOWN
O, LORD, O, MY LORD
KEEP ME FROM SINKIN' DOWN...

MANNERS. Cut, relax, at ease!

MILLIE. *(Brushes lint from her skirt.)* I'll have to bring work clothes.

SHELDON. *(To* **MILLIE.***)* I almost hit the number yesterday.

MILLIE. I'm glad you didn't.

(**BILL** *crosses to* **MANNERS***; we hear snatches of their conversation as the others cross-talk.*)

JUDY. *(To* **JOHN.***)* Did you finish my book?

(**JOHN** *claps his hand to his forehead in a typical* **MANNERS** *gesture.*)

BILL. *(A light conference on* **WILETTA.***)* A line of physical action might...

SHELDON. *(To* **MILLIE.***)* I almost got an apartment.

MANNERS. Limited emotional capacity.

MILLIE. *(To* **SHELDON.***) Almost* doesn't mean a thing.

MANNERS. Well, it's coming. Sheldon, I like what's happening.

SHELDON. Thank you, does he give himself up to Judge Willis and get saved?

MANNERS. *(Flabbergasted, as are* **JOHN, JUDY, BILL,** *and* **EDDIE.***)* Shel, haven't you read it? Haven't you heard us read it?

SHELDON. No, I just go over and over my own lines, I ain't in the last of the third act.

JUDY. Are my motivations coming through?

MANNERS. Yeah, forget it. Sit down, Sheldon...just for you... Renard drives him toward jail, deputies stop them on the way, someone shoots and kills Job as he tries to escape, afterward they find out he was innocent, Renard makes everyone feel like a dog...they realize they were wrong and so forth.

SHELDON. And so forth.

MANNERS. He makes them realize that lynching is wrong.

(*He refers to his notes.*)

SHELDON. *(To* **WILETTA.***)* What was he innocent of?

WILETTA. I don't know.

JOHN. About the voting.

SHELDON. Uh-uh, he was guilty of that 'cause he done confessed.

MANNERS. Innocent of wrongdoing, Sheldon.

SHELDON. Uh-huh, oh, yeah.

MANNERS. Yale, you're on the right track. John, what can I say? You're great. Millie, you're growing, gaining command... I begin to feel an inner as well as the outer rendering.

JOHN. If we could run the sequence without interruption.

SHELDON. Yeah, then we would motorate and all that.

MANNERS. *(To* **WILETTA**.*)* Dear heart, I've got to tell you...

WILETTA. I ain't so hot.

MANNERS. Don't be sensitive, let me help you, will you?

WILETTA. *(Trying to handle* **MANNERS** *in the same way as* **JOHN** *and* **JUDY**.*)* I know my relations and motivations may not be just so...

SHELDON. *(Wisely.)* Uh-huh, *motivation*, that's the thing.

WILETTA. They not right and I think I know why...

MANNERS. Darling, that's my department, will you listen?

> *(***JOHN** *is self-conscious about* **WILETTA** *and* **SHELDON**. *He is ashamed of them and has reached the point where he exchanges knowing looks with* **BILL**, **EDDIE**, *and* **MANNERS**.*)*

WILETTA. You don't ever listen to me. You hear the others but not me. And it's 'cause of the school. 'Cause they know 'bout justifyin' and the antagonist... I never studied that, so you don't want to hear me, that's all right.

JUDY. *(Stricken to the heart.)* Oh, don't say that.

SHELDON. He listen to me, and I ain't had it.

JOHN. *(Starts to put his arm around* **WILETTA.***)* Oh, Wiletta...

WILETTA. *(Moving away from him.)* Oh, go on.

MANNERS. Wiletta, dear, I'm sorry if I've complicated things. I'll make it as clear as I can. You are pretending to act and I can see through your pretense. I want truth. What is truth? Truth is simply whatever you can bring yourself to believe, that is all. You must have integrity about your work...a sense of...well, sense.

WILETTA. I'm tryin' to lose myself like you say but...

JOHN. *(Wants to help but is afraid to interrupt.)* Oh, no...

MANNERS. *(Sternly.)* You can't lose yourself, you are you... and you can't get away. You, Wiletta, must relate.

SHELDON. That's what I do.

WILETTA. I don't see why the boy couldn't get away...it's the killin' that...something's wrong. I may be in fast company but I got as much integrity as any. I didn't start workin' no yesterday.

MANNERS. No, Wiletta, no self-pity. Look, he can't escape this death. We want audience sympathy. We have a very subtle point to make, very subtle...

BILL. I hate the kind of play that bangs you over the head with the message. Keep it subtle.

MANNERS. *(Getting very basic.)* We don't want to antagonize the audience.

WILETTA. It'll make 'em mad if he gets away?

MANNERS. This is a simple, sweet, lovable guy. Sheldon, does it offend you that he gives himself up to Judge Willis?

SHELDON. No, not if that's how they do.

MANNERS. We're making one beautiful, clear point...
violence is wrong.

WILETTA. My friend, Miss Green, say she don't see why
they act like this.

> (JOHN *thinks he knows how to handle*
> WILETTA. *He is about to burst with an idea.*
> MANNERS *decides to let* JOHN *wade in.*)

JOHN. Look, think of the intellectual level here...they're
underprivileged, uneducated...

WILETTA. (*Letting* JOHN *know he's treading on thin ice.*)
Look out, you ain't so smart.

JOHN. (*Showing so much of* MANNERS.) They've probably
never seen a movie or television...never used a
telephone. They...they're not like us. They're good,
kind, folksy people...but they're ignorant, they just
don't know.

WILETTA. You ain't the director.

SHELDON. (*To* JOHN.) You better hush.

MANNERS. We're dealing with simple, backward people
but they're human beings.

WILETTA. 'Cause they colored, you tellin' me they're human
bein's... I *know* I'm a human bein'... Listen here...

MANNERS. I will not listen! It does not matter to me that
they're Negroes. Black, white, green, or purple, I maintain
there is only one race...the human race.

> (SHELDON *bursts into applause.*)

MILLIE. That's true.

MANNERS. Don't think "Negro," think "people."

SHELDON. Let's stop segregatin' ourselves.

JOHN. *(To* **WILETTA.***)* I didn't mean any harm, you don't understand...

BILL. *(To* **MILLIE,** *as he looks heavenward and acts out his weariness.)* Oh, honey child!

MILLIE. Don't call me no damn honey child!

BILL. Well, is my face red?

MILLIE. Yeah, and on you it looks good.

MANNERS. What's going on?

MILLIE. Honey child.

WILETTA. *(Mumbling as all dialogue falls pell-mell.)* Justify.

BILL. *(With great resignation.)* Trying to be friendly.

WILETTA. Justify.

MILLIE. Get friendly with someone else.

MANNERS. May we have order!

SHELDON. *(In a terrible flash of temper.)* That's why they don't do more colored shows! Always fightin'! Everybody hush, let this man direct! He don't even have to be here! Right now he could be out in Hollywood in the middle of a big investigation!

EDDIE. The word is production!

SHELDON. That's what I said, production.

EDDIE. No, you didn't.

SHELDON. What'd I say?

MANNERS. *(Bangs table.)* I will not countenance another outbreak of this nature. I say to each and every one of you... I am in charge and I'll thank you to remember it. I've been much too lax, too informal. Well, it doesn't work. There's going to be order.

WILETTA. I was only sayin'...

MANNERS. I said *everyone*! My patience is at an end. I demand your concentrated attention. It's as simple as A, B, C, if you will apply yourselves. The threat of this horrible violence throws you into cold, stark fear. It's a perfectly human emotion, anyone would feel it. I'm not asking you to dream up some fantastic horror...it's a lynching. We've never actually seen such a thing, thank God...but allow your imagination to soar, to take hold of it...think.

SHELDON. I seen one.

MANNERS. *(Can't believe he heard right.)* What?

BILL. What did you see?

SHELDON. A lynchin', when I was a little boy 'bout nine years old.

JUDY. Oh, no.

WILETTA. How did it happen? Tell me, Sheldon, did you really?

MANNERS. Would it help you to know, Wiletta?

WILETTA. I...guess... I don't know.

BILL. *(Not eager to hear about it.)* Will it bother you, Sheldon? It could be wrong for him... I don't know...

(**EDDIE** *gives* **MANNERS** *a doubtful look.*)

MILLIE. That must be something to see.

MANNERS. *(With a sigh.)* Go on, Sheldon.

(**MANNERS** *watches* **CAST** *reactions.*)

SHELDON. I think it was on a Saturday, yeah, it had to be or else-wise I woulda been in the field with my ma and pa.

WILETTA. What field?

SHELDON. The cotton field. My ma said I was too little to go every day, but some of 'em younger'n me was out there all the time. My grandma was home with me...

(**SHELDON** *thinks of his grandma and almost forgets his story.*)

WILETTA. What about the lynchin'?

SHELDON. It was Saturday and rainin' a sort of sifty rain. I was standin' at the window watchin' the lilac bush wavin' in the wind. A sound come to my ears like bees hummin'...was voices comin' closer and closer, screamin' and cursin'. My granny tried to pull me from the window. "Come on, chile," she said, "they gonna kill us all...hide!" But I was fightin' to keep from goin' with her, scared to go in the dark closet.

(**JUDY** *places her hands over her ears and bows her head.*)

The screamin' comin' closer and closer...and the screamin' was laughin'... Lord, how they was laughin'... louder and louder.

(*He rises and puts in his best performance to date. He raises one hand and creates a stillness... Everyone is spellbound.*)

Hush! Then I hear wagon wheels bumpin' over the wet, stony road, chains clankin'. Man drivin' the wagon, beatin' the horse... Ahhhhhhhh! Ahhhhhhhh! Horse just pullin' along...and then I saw it! Chained to the back of the wagon, draggin' and bumpin' along...

(*He opens his arms wide.*)

The arms of it stretched out...a burnt, naked thing...a burnt, naked thing that once was a man...and I started to scream but no sound come out...just a screamin' but no sound...

(*He lowers his arms and brings the company back to the present.*)

That was Mr. Morris that they killed. Mr. Morris. I remember one time he come to our house and was laughin' and talkin' about everything...and he give us a fruitcake that his wife made. Folks said he was crazy...you know, 'bout talkin' back...quick to speak his mind. I left there when I was seventeen. I don't want to live in no place like that.

MANNERS. When I hear of barbarism...I feel so wretched, so guilty.

SHELDON. Don't feel that way. You wouldn't kill nobody and do 'em like that...would you?

MANNERS. *(Hurt by the question.)* No, Sheldon.

SHELDON. That's what I know.

> (**BILL** *crosses and rests his hand on* **SHELDON***'s shoulder.* **SHELDON** *flinches because he hadn't noticed* **BILL***'s approach.)*

Oh! I didn't see you. Did I help y'all by tellin' that story?

MANNERS. It was quite an experience. I'm shot. Break for lunch, we'll pick up in an hour, have a good afternoon session.

MILLIE. Makes me feel like goin' out in the street and crackin' heads.

JUDY. *(Shocked.)* Oh!

EDDIE. Makes my blood boil...but what can you do?

MANNERS. We're doing a play.

MILLIE. *(To* **JUDY***.)* I'm starved. You promised to show us that Italian place.

JUDY. *(Surprised that* **MILLIE** *no longer feels violent.)* Why...sure, I'd love to. Let's have a festive lunch, with wine!

SHELDON. Yeah, that wine that comes in a straw bottle.

JUDY. Imported wine.

MILLIE. And chicken cacciatore...let's live!

> (**WILETTA** *crosses to* **MANNERS** *while others are getting coats; she has hit on a scheme to make* **MANNERS** *see her point.*)

WILETTA. Look here, I ain't gonna let you get mad with me. You supposed to be my buddy.

JOHN. Let's go!

> (**MANNERS** *opens his arms to* **WILETTA.**)

MANNERS. I'm glad you said that. You're my sweetheart.

MILLIE. Bill, how about you?

BILL. (*Places his hand on his stomach.*) The Italian place. Okay, count me in.

EDDIE. (*Stacking scripts.*) I want a king-size dish of clams... raw ones.

WILETTA. Wouldn't it be nice if the mother could say, "Son, you right! I don't want to send you outta here but I don't know what to do..."

MANNERS. Darling, darling...no.

MILLIE. Wiletta, get a move on.

WILETTA. Or else she says, "Run for it, Job!" and then they catch him like that...he's dead *anyway*, see?

MANNERS. (*Trying to cover his annoyance.*) It's not the script, it's *you*. Bronson does the writing, you do the acting, it's that simple.

SHELDON. One race, the human race. I like that.

JUDY. Veal parmesan with oodles and oodles of cheese!

WILETTA. I was just thinkin' if I could...

MANNERS. (*Indicating script.*) Address yourself to this.

JUDY. (*To* **JOHN.**) Bring my book tomorrow.

JOHN. Cross my heart.

WILETTA. I just wanted to talk about...

MANNERS. You are going to get a spanking.

> *(He leaves with* **EDDIE** *and others.)*

MILLIE. Wiletta, come on!

WILETTA. *(Abruptly.)* I... I'll be there later.

MILLIE. *(Miffed by the short answer.)* Suit yourself.

JUDY. *(To* **WILETTA.***)* It's on the corner of Sixth Avenue on this side of the street.

JOHN. Correction. Correction, Avenue of the Americas.

> *(Laughter from* **MANNERS, MILLIE, SHELDON,** *and* **BILL** *offstage.)*

JUDY. *(Posturing in her best theatrical style.)* But no one, absolutely no one ever says it. He's impossible, absolutely impossible!

WILETTA. Oh, ain't he though.

> *(***JOHN** *bows to* **JUDY** *and indicates that she goes first.)*

JOHN. Dear Gaston, Alphonse will follow.

WILETTA. John, I told you everything wrong 'cause I didn't know better, that's the size of it. No fool like an old fool. You right, don't make sense to be bowin' and scrapin' and Tommin'... No, don't pay no attention to what I said.

JOHN. *(Completely* **MANNERS.***)* Wiletta, my dear, you're my sweetheart, I love you madly and I think you're wonderfully magnificent!

> *(***JUDY** *suddenly notices his posturing and hers; she feels silly. She laughs, laughter bordering on tears.)*

JUDY. John, you're a puppet with strings attached and so am I. Everyone's a stranger and I'm the strangest of all.

(She quickly leaves.)

JOHN. Wiletta, don't forget to come over!

*(He follows **JUDY**.)*

WILETTA. *(Paces up and down, tries doing her lines aloud.)* Only one thing to do, give yourself up! Give yourself up...give up...give up...give up...give up...give up.

> *(Lights whirl and flicker. Blues record comes in loud, then down, lights flicker to indicate passage of time.* **WILETTA** is gone. Stage is empty.)*
>
> *(**BILL** enters, removing his coat. He has a slight attack of indigestion and belches his disapproval of pizza pie. **OTHERS** can be heard laughing and talking offstage.)*

BILL. Ohhhhhh, ahhhhh...

> *(**MANNERS** enters with **EDDIE**. **EDDIE** proceeds to the table and script. **MANNERS** is just getting over the effects of a good laugh...but his mirth suddenly fades as he crosses to **BILL**.)*

MANNERS. I am sorry you felt compelled to tell that joke about the colored minister and the stolen chicken.

BILL. Trying to be friendly... I don't know... I even ate pizza.

EDDIE. I always *think*...think first, is this the right thing to say, would I want anyone to say this to me?

---

*A license to produce *Trouble in Mind* does not include a performance license for any third-party or copyrighted music. Licensees should create an original composition or use music in the public domain. For further information, please see the Music and Third-Party Materials Use Note on page iii.

(Burst of laughter from offstage.)

BILL. Oh, you're so noble, you give me a pain in the ass. Love thy neighbor as thyself, now I ask you, is that a reasonable request?

MANNERS. *(For fear the others will hear.)* All right. Knock it off.

BILL. Okay, I said I was sorry, but for what... I'll never know.

> (SHELDON, MILLIE, JUDY, *and* JOHN *enter in a hilarious mood.* JUDY *is definitely feeling the wine.* SHELDON *is supplying the fun.)*

SHELDON. Sure, I was workin' my hind parts off... Superintendent of the buildin'...

JOHN. But the tenants, Shel! That's a riot!

SHELDON. One day a man came along and offered me fifty dollars a week just to walk across the stage real slow. *(Mimics his acting role.)* Sure, I took it! Hard as I worked I was glad to slow down!

> (OTHERS *laugh.)*

JUDY. *(Holds her head.)* Ohhhhhh, that wine.

MILLIE. Wasn't it good? I wanna get a whole *case* of it for the holidays. All that I have to do! My liquors, wreathes, presents, cards... I'm gonna buy my husband a tape recorder.

JUDY. *(To* JOHN.*)* I'm sorry I hurt your feelings but you are a little puppet, and I'm a little puppet, and all the world...

> (She impresses the lesson by tapping JOHN *on his chest.)*

MANNERS. Judy, I want to go over something with you...

JUDY. No, you don't...you're afraid I'm going to...hic. 'Fraid I'll go overboard on the friendship deal and *com*plicate matters...complications...

MANNERS. Two or three glasses of wine, she's delirious. Do you want some black coffee?

JUDY. No, no, I only have hiccups.

MILLIE. *(To* **JOHN.***)* Which would you rather have, a tape recorder or a camera?

JOHN. I don't know.

SHELDON. I'd rather have some money, make mine cash.

MANNERS. *(To* **JUDY.***)* Why don't you sit down and get yourself together?

> *(***JUDY** *sits.)*

JOHN. *(To* **MANNERS.***)* I...I think I have some questions about Wiletta and the third act.

MANNERS. It's settled, don't worry, John, she's got it straight.

JOHN. I know but it seems...

MANNERS. Hoskins sat out front yesterday afternoon. He's mad about you. First thing he says, "Somebody's going to try and steal that boy from us."

JOHN. *(Very pleased.)* I'm glad I didn't know he was there.

MANNERS. Eddie, call it, will you? Okay, attention!

EDDIE. Beginning of the third.

> *(***COMPANY** *quiets down, opens scripts.* **WILETTA** *enters.)*

MANNERS. You're late.

WILETTA. I know it. *(To* **MILLIE.***)* I had a bowl of soup and was able to relate to it and justify, no trouble at all. *(To* **MANNERS.***)* I'm not gonna take up your time now but I wanta see you at the end of the afternoon.

MANNERS. Well... I... I'll let you know...we'll see.

WILETTA. It's important.

MANNERS. *(Ignoring her and addressing entire* **COMPANY.***)* Attention, I want to touch on a corner of what we did this morning and then we'll highlight the rest of three!

(**ACTORS** *rise and start for places.*)

John, top of page four.

JOHN. When a man has a decent word to say for us down here, I gonna vote for him.

WILETTA. *(With real force; she is lecturing him rather than scolding.)* A decent word? And that's all you ever gonna get out of him. Dammit, he ain't gonna win no how. They done said he ain't and they gonna see to it! And you gonna be dead for a decent word.

MANNERS. *(To* **EDDIE.***)* This is deliberate.

JOHN. I gotta go, I ain't gonna wait to be killed.

WILETTA. There's only one right thing to do. You got to go and give yourself up.

JOHN. I ain't done nothin'.

JUDY. My father will have Judge Willis put you in the county jail where you'll be safe.

(**MANNERS** *is quite disheartened.*)

WILETTA. Job, she's tryin' to help us.

JUDY. I'm thinking of the others even if you aren't. I don't want murder in this community.

WILETTA. Boy, get down on your knees.

(**JOHN** *falls to his knees.*)

Oh, Lord touch this boy's heart. Reach him tonight, take the fear and hatred out of his soul!

SHELDON. Hmmmmmm, mmmmmm, mmmmmmmm...

MILLIE. Mercy, Lord.

JOHN. Stop, I can't stand any more...

> (**WILETTA** *tries to raise* **JOHN.**)

MANNERS. No, keep him on his knees.

JOHN. I can't stand any more...whatever you say...

> (*Again,* **WILETTA** *tries to raise him.*)

SHELDON. (*To* **WILETTA.**) He say keep him on his knees.

WILETTA. Aw, get up off the floor, wallowin' around like that.

> (*Everyone is shocked.*)

MANNERS. Wiletta, this is not the time or place to...

WILETTA. All that crawlin' and goin' on before me...hell, I ain't the one tryin' to lynch him. This ain't sayin' nothin', don't make sense. Talkin' 'bout the truth is anything I can believe...well, I don't believe this.

MANNERS. I will not allow you to interrupt in this disorganized manner.

WILETTA. You been askin' me what I think and where things come from and how come I thought it and all that. Where is this comin' from?

> (**COMPANY** *murmuring in the background.*)

Tell me, why this boy's people turned against him? Why we sendin' him out into the teeth of a lynch mob? I'm his mother and I'm sendin' him to his death. This is a lie.

JOHN. But his mother doesn't understand... There have been cases of men dragged from their homes...

WILETTA. But they was *dragged*...they come with guns and dragged 'em out. They weren't sent to be killed by their mama. The writer wants the damn white man to be the hero – and me the villain.

MILLIE. I think we're all tired.

SHELDON. Outta order, outta order, you outta order. This ain't the time.

MANNERS. Wiletta, there are some who may deserve this from you but I'm not the one.

SHELDON. No, you ain't.

MANNERS. As long as I've known you, you've never given me any trouble.

WILETTA. And that's what's the matter.

MANNERS. What do you want to do when the mob comes after Job? Shoot it out? That's sheer violence.

WILETTA. Yeah, kill my child and call me violent, that's what comes of all the justifyin'.

MANNERS. I'm going to tell you something you've never known before now. Remember the last picture we made together? You played a character part. I had to sweat blood, stayed up all night with the writers... getting them to change a stereotype mammy role into something decent for you...

WILETTA. And when you got through, dammit, it was still a mammy part. Character part! Lemme tell you 'bout them character parts.

(She startles COMPANY by falling into character.) "Oh, Miss Wentworth, I'm so distress, I don't know what to do."

(Falls out of character.) Always distressed and don't know a damn thing to do!

(Back into character.) "It's 'bout my son, he's a good boy but he's got notions that's gonna get him in trouble."

(Out of character.) Our sons always got notions that they as good as anybody else, and we always askin' the white folks we work for to change their minds for 'em! We got husbands too, you may not see 'em but you hear 'bout 'em in those character parts.

(In character.) "I don't know why I stays with that man, he won't work, he won't come home, I don't know why I loves him, guess it's 'cause he keeps me laughin' all the time."

(Out of character.) You ever hear of a lazy, no-good, two-timin' man keepin' a woman laughin' all the time? Character part!

A baby in my arms. *(In character.)* "You're my little angel, and just like I raised your mama, I'm gonna raise you to be a little lady."

(Making up her own act.) Dear little baby of the folks I work for, I got a present for you...my whole damn life! I'm handin' it over to you and your ma and pa. If you got no money to pay me, I wanna stay anyhow, my pleasure is to wait on you forever. To hell with my children and hooray for you!

(Out of character.) You stayin' up all night fixin' up character parts for me! Givin' 'em what you call dignity! Dignity! You know what your dignity is? A old black straw hat with a flower stickin' up in front, hands folded 'cross my stomach, sayin' the same damn fool things...only nice and easy and proper!

(In character.) "I know it's none of my business, Mrs. Sanders, but I just got to say it. You haven't been yourself lately and it grieves me to see you eatin' your heart out 'bout Mr. John. I try to pretend I don't see it, but I do. It's almost more than a body can stand."

MANNERS. I'm sorry you've had to play maids but it's not my fault...

WILETTA. They're not maids. What you call maids aren't even people! I got news for you. We don't give a damn 'bout Mr. John or Mr. Renard either. I don't sit down and eat with 'em and I ain't sittin' up nights worryin' 'bout 'em. Dignity! All them lyin' pictures I seen with white folks pretendin' they passin' for white? When they wanta show a colored girl passin', they go and get this child to do it. *(Points to* **JUDY.***)*

MILLIE. Exactly.

WILETTA. Who gets to play the Indian Chief? Look close and you'll see he's got blue eyes, and you gonna tell me 'bout truth and justifyin'? And don't dare be BLACK ...then you got to scratch your head *(Demonstrates.)* every time you start to think...plowin' up thoughts. Justify! Oh, I'm holdin' class today.

BILL. Wiletta, I've had to do roles that I found objectionable.

WILETTA. I'm wise. But you don't give a damn 'cause a lynch mob ain't after you! I know what you play... turnin' into a fanged wolf when the moon is full, turnin' into a vampire bat, a blood-sucker! You *had* to go to school to justify that. On that tee-vee box y'all shootin' down each other every night, all night long. Shootin' and kissin', that's all you know...how big is your bust and murder, murder, murder. Yes indeed, that's *your* stereotype. Suit yourself, but I'm sicka mine. I'm full, my cup runneth over. *(Points to script.)* Would you... could you do this to a son of yours?

MANNERS. She places him in the hands of Judge Willis and...

WILETTA. And I tell you she knows better.

BILL. It's only because she trusts and believes. Couldn't you trust and believe in Al?

MANNERS. Bill, please.

WILETTA. No, I wouldn't trust him with my son's life.

MANNERS. Thank you.

SHELDON. She don't mean it.

WILETTA. Judge Willis! Why don't his people help him?

MANNERS. The story goes a certain way and...

WILETTA. It oughta go another way.

ENTIRE COMPANY. *(In unison.)* Talk about it later... We're all tired... Yes... We need a rest... Sometimes your own won't help you.

MANNERS. Leave her alone!

> *(He is on fire now. He loves the challenge of this conflict and is determined to win the battle. He must win.)*

Why this great fear of death? Christ died for something and...

WILETTA. Sure, they came and got him and hauled him off to jail. His mother didn't turn him in, in fact, the one who did it was one of them so-called friends.

MANNERS. His death proved something. Job's death brings him the lesson.

WILETTA. That they should stop lynchin' *innocent* men! Fine thing! Lynch the guilty, is that the idea? The dark-skinned Oliver Twist. *(Points to* **JOHN.**) That's you. Yeah, I mean, you got to go to school to justify this!

MANNERS. Wiletta, I've listened. I've heard you out...

WILETTA. *(To* **SHELDON.**) And you echoin' every damn word he says – "Keep him on his knees."

MANNERS. I've heard you out and even though you think you know more than the author...

WILETTA. You don't want to hear. You are a prejudiced man, a prejudiced racist.

(Gasp from **COMPANY.***)*

MANNERS. *(Caught off guard.)* I will not accept that from you or anyone else.

WILETTA. I told this boy to laugh and grin at everything you said, well... I ain't laughin'.

MANNERS. While you give me hell-up-the-river, I'm supposed to stand here and take it with a tolerance beyond human endurance. I'm white! You think it's so wonderful to be white? I've got troubles up to here! But I don't expect anyone to hand me anything and it's high time you got rid of that notion. No, I never worked in a cotton field. I didn't. I was raised in a nice, comfortable, nine-room house in the Midwest...and I learned to say nigger, kike, sheeny, spic, dago, wop, and chink... I hear 'em plenty! I was raised by a sweet, dear, kind old aunt, who spent her time gathering funds for missionaries...but she almost turned our town upside down when Mexicans moved in on our block. I know about troubles...my own! I've never been *handed* any gifts. Oh, it's so grand to be white! I had to crawl and knuckle under step by step. What I want and what I believe, indeed! I directed blood, guts, fistfights, bedroom farces, and the lowest kind of dirtied-up sex until I earned the respect of this business.

WILETTA. But would you send your son out to...

MANNERS. I proclaim this National Truth Week! Whites! You think we belong to one great, grand fraternity? They stole and snatched from me for years, and I'm a club member! Ever hear of an idea man? They picked my brains! They stripped me! They threw me cash and I let the credit go! My brains milked, while somebody else climbed on my back to take bows. But I didn't beg for mercy...why waste your breath? I learned one thing that's the only damned truth worth knowing... you get nothin' for nothin', but nothin'! No favors, no dreams served up on silver platters. Now...finally I get something for all of us...but it's not enough for you! I'm prejudiced! Get wise, there's damned few of us interested in putting on a colored show at all, much less one that's going to say anything. It's rough out here, it's a hard world! Do you think I can stick my neck out by telling the truth about you? There are billions of things that *can't be said*...do you follow me, billions! Where the hell do you think I can raise a hundred thousand dollars to tell the unvarnished truth?

(Picks up the script and waves it.)

So, maybe it's a lie...but it's one of the finest lies you'll come across for a damned long time! Here's bitter news, since you're livin' off truth... The American public is not ready to see you the way you want to be seen because, one, they don't believe it, two, they don't want to believe it, and three, they're convinced they're superior – and that, my friend, is why Carrie and Renard have to carry the ball! Get it? Now you wise up and aim for the soft spot in that American heart, let 'em pity you, make 'em weep buckets, be helpless, make 'em feel so damned sorry for you that they'll lend a hand in easing up the pressure. You've got a free ride. Coast, baby, coast.

WILETTA. Would you send your son out to be murdered?

MANNERS. *(So wound up, he answers without thinking.)* Don't compare yourself to me! What goes for my son doesn't necessarily go for yours! Don't compare him... *(Points to **JOHN**.)* with three strikes against him, don't compare him with my son, they've got nothing in common...not a goddamn thing!

> *(He realizes what he has said, also that he has lost company sympathy. He is utterly confused and embarrassed by his own statement.)*

I tried to make it clear.

JOHN. It is clear.

> (**MANNERS** *quickly exits to the dressing room.*
> **EDDIE** *follows him.* **JUDY** *has an impulse to*
> *follow.)*

BILL. No, leave him alone.

JOHN. *(To* **WILETTA.***)* I feel like a fool… Hmmph. "Don't
think Negro, think *people.*"

SHELDON. *(To* **BILL.***)* You think he means we're fired?

BILL. I don't know… I don't know…

MILLIE. Wiletta, this should have been discussed with
everyone first.

SHELDON. Done talked yourself out of a job.

BILL. Shel, you don't know that.

> (*During the following scene,* **SHELDON** *is*
> *more active and dynamic than ever before.)*

SHELDON. Well, he didn't go out there to bake her no birthday
cake.

> (**JUDY** *is quietly crying.)*

MILLIE. We got all the truth we bargained for and then some.

WILETTA. Yes, I spoke my mind and he spoke his.

BILL. We have a company representative, Sheldon is the
deputy. Any complaints we have should be handled
in an orderly manner. Equity has rules, the rule book
says…

SHELDON. I left my rule book home. Furthermore, I don't
think I want to be the deputy.

MILLIE. He was dead right about some things but I didn't
appreciate that *last* remark.

SHELDON. *(To* **WILETTA.***)* You can't spit in somebody's eye and tell 'em you was washin' it out.

BILL. Sheldon, now is not the time to resign.

SHELDON. *(Taking charge.)* All right, I'm tryin' to lead 'em, tryin' to play peacemaker. Shame on y'all! Look at the U.N.!

MILLIE. The U.N.?

SHELDON. Yes, the United Nations. You think they run their business by blabbin' everything they think? No! They talk sweet and polite 'til they can outslick the next feller. Wisdom! The greatest gift in the world, they got it! *(To* **WILETTA.***)* Way you talked, I thought you had the 'tomic bomb.

WILETTA. I'm sick of people signifyin' we got no sense.

SHELDON. I know. I'm the only man in the house and what am I doin'? Whittlin' a doggone stick. But I whittled it, didn't I? I can't write a play and I got no money to put one on... Yes! I'm gonna whittle my stick!

(He stamps his foot to emphasize the point.)

JOHN. *(Very noble and very worried.)* How do you go about putting in a notice?

SHELDON. *(To* **JOHN.***)* Hold on 'til I get to you.

(To **WILETTA.***)* Now, when he gets back here, you be sure and tell him.

WILETTA. Tell him what?

SHELDON. Damn, tell him you *sorry*.

BILL. Oh, he doesn't want that.

WILETTA. Shame on him if he does.

MILLIE. I don't want to spend the rest of the day wondering why he walked out.

WILETTA. I'm playin' a leadin' part and I want this script changed or else.

SHELDON. Hush up, before the man hears you.

MILLIE. Just make sure you're not the one to tell him. You're a great one for runnin' to management and telling your guts.

SHELDON. I never told management nothin', anybody say I did is lyin'.

JUDY. Let's ask for a *quiet* talk to straighten things out.

BILL. No. This is between Wiletta and Manners and I'm sure they can...

JOHN. We all ought to show some integrity.

SHELDON. Integrity...got us in a big mess.

MILLIE. *(To* **JOHN.***)* You can't put in your notice until after opening night. You've got to follow Equity rules...

SHELDON. Yeah, he's trying to defy the union.

WILETTA. *(Thumping the script.)* This is a damn lie.

MILLIE. But you can't tell people what to write, that's censorship.

SHELDON. *(To* **WILETTA.***)* And that's another point in your disfavor.

JOHN. They can write what they want but we don't have to do it.

SHELDON. You outta order!

BILL. *(To* **JOHN.***)* Oh, don't keep stirring it up, heaping on coals...

JUDY. Wiletta, maybe if we appeal to Mr. Hoskins or Mr. Bronson...

SHELDON. The producer and the author ain't gonna listen to her, after all...they white same as Manners.

JUDY. I resent that!

BILL. I do too, Shel.

JUDY. I've had an awful lot of digs thrown on me...remarks about white, white...and I do resent it.

JOHN. *(To* **JUDY.***)* He means what can you expect from Sheldon. *(To* **SHELDON.***)* Sheldon.

BILL. *(To* **JUDY.***)* I'm glad you said that.

SHELDON. I'm sorry, I won't say nothin' 'bout white. *(To* **WILETTA.***)* Look here, Hoskins, Manners, and Bronson...they got things in...er...common, you know what I mean?

WILETTA. Leave me alone...and suit yourselves.

MILLIE. I know what's right but I need this job.

SHELDON. There you go...talk.

WILETTA. Thought your husband doesn't want you to work.

MILLIE. He doesn't but I have to anyway.

JUDY. But you'll still be in New York. If this falls through I'll have to go back to Bridgeport...before I even get started.

JOHN. Maybe I'll never get another job.

MILLIE. Like Al Manners says, there's more to this life than the truth. *(To* **JUDY.***)* You'll have to go to Bridgeport. Oh, how I wish I had a Bridgeport.

BILL. Okay, enough, *I'm* the villain. I get plenty of work, forgive me.

JUDY. Life scares me, honestly it does.

SHELDON. When you kick up a disturbance, the man's in his rights to call the cops...police car will come rollin' up here, next thing you know...you'll be servin' time.

MILLIE. Don't threaten her!

JOHN. Why don't you call a cop *for* him...try it.

(**HENRY** *enters, carrying a paper bag.*)

HENRY. I got Mr. Manners some nice danish, cheese, and prune.

MILLIE. He can't eat it right now...leave it there.

(**EDDIE** *enters with a shaken but stern attitude.*)

EDDIE. Attention company. You are all dismissed for the day. I'll telephone about tomorrow's rehearsal.

SHELDON. Tell Mr. Manners I'm gonna memorize my first act.

(**EDDIE** *exits, and* **SHELDON** *talks to* **COMPANY.***)

I still owe the doctor money...and I can't lift no heavy boxes or be scrubbin' no floors. If I was a drinkin' man I'd get drunk.

MILLIE. Tomorrow is another day. Maybe everybody will be in better condition to...talk...just talk it all out. Let's go to the corner for coffee and a calm chat. *(Suddenly solicitous with* **JUDY.***)* How about you, honey, wouldn't you like to relax and look over the situation? Bill?

BILL. I have to study for my soap opera...but thanks.

JUDY. Yes, let's go talk.

MILLIE. John? Wiletta, honey, let's go for coffee.

WILETTA. I'll be there after a while. Go on.

JOHN. We couldn't go without you.

SHELDON. We don't want to leave you by yourself in this old theater.

WILETTA. There are times when you got to be alone. *This is mine.*

(JOHN indicates that they should leave. MILLIE, SHELDON, JUDY, JOHN, and BILL exit.)

HENRY. Are you cryin'?

WILETTA. Yes.

HENRY. Ah, don't do that. It's too nice a day.

(He sits near the tape recorder.)

I started to throw coffee at him that time when he kicked up a fuss, but you got to take a lotta things in this life.

WILETTA. Divide and conquer...that's the way they get the upper hand. A telephone call for tomorrow's rehearsal... they won't call me... But I'm gonna show up any damn way. The next move is his. He'll have to fire me.

HENRY. Whatcha say?

WILETTA. We have to go further and do better.

HENRY. That's a good one. I'll remember that. What's on this, music?

(WILETTA turns the machine on and down. The applause plays.)

WILETTA. Canned applause. When you need a bit of instant praise...you turn it on...and there you are.

(HENRY tries it.)

HENRY. Canned applause. They got everything these days. Time flies. I bet you can't guess how old I am.

WILETTA. Not more than sixty.

HENRY. I'm seventy-eight.

WILETTA. Imagine that. A fine-lookin' man like you.

(Sound of police siren in street.)

HENRY. What's that?

WILETTA. Police siren.

HENRY. They got a fire engine house next to where I live. God-in-heaven, you never heard such a noise...and I'm kinda deaf... Didn't know that, did you?

WILETTA. No, I didn't. Some live by what they call great truths. Henry, I've always wanted to do somethin' real grand...in the theater...to stand forth at my best...to stand up here and do anything I want...

HENRY. Like my father...he was in vaudeville...doin' the soft-shoe and tippin' his hat to the ladies...

WILETTA. Yes, somethin' grand.

HENRY. *(Adjusting the tape recorder to play applause.)* Do it...do it. I'm the audience.

WILETTA. I don't remember anything grand... I can't recall.

HENRY. Say somethin' from the Bible...like the twenty-third psalm.

WILETTA. Oh, I know.

> *(She comes downstage and recites beautifully from Psalm 133:)*

Behold how good and how pleasant it is for brethren to dwell together in unity. It is like the precious ointment upon the head, that ran down upon the beard, even Aaron's beard; that went down to the skirts of his garment; as the dew of Hermon, and as the dew that descended upon the mountains of Zion; for there the Lord commanded the blessing, even life forevermore.

> *(**HENRY** turns on applause as **WILETTA** stands tall for the curtain.)*

End of Play

Milton Keynes UK
Ingram Content Group UK Ltd.
UKHW021820130923
428619UK00010B/453